FIRST LOVE

BY

MELISSA JOHNS

FIRST LOVE

MELISSA JOHNS

Copyright © 2012

Dedication

This book is dedicated to my 7th & 8th grade teacher, Mrs. Susan Brese. She gave me the inspiration to write whatever was in my heart and gave me the strength to put it on paper.

Also, my wonderful husband, Mark for dealing with me as I finally started my dream.

Preface

You never forget your first love, even if you don't end up with them. This tale will remind you of your story.

TABLE OF CONTENTS

NEW LIFE

Have you ever felt lost or just out of place? I'm feeling that way right now as I stand in the lobby of my new high school. I should be thinking about where my first class is or if anyone wants to be friends with me but I'm not, I'm worried that I made the wrong decision about moving to New York and not sure if will I fit in. I'm eighteen years old and I'm starting over in a new school and a new life.

I moved here from Texas during the summer. My home life wasn't great. My father remarried and I couldn't stand his new wife. She thought I was a nuisance and I monopolized all his time. She knew I saw right through her. With a blink of an eye, she got whatever she wanted. I couldn't handle it anymore and decided it was a good time to spend some time with my mother.

My mom left years ago and I didn't want to leave so I was able to live with my dad. I always felt horrible about that decision because I do love my mother and wanted to be with her. But, at the time I was too scared to move away from what I knew. So, my parents came to an understanding and I was able to stay in Texas.

So, I decided it was time to move to Buffalo, New York. I received no arguments from my step-mother. I'm sure she threw a party when I left. I arrived in late summer and my mother enrolled me into my senior year of high school at the local public school, which is where I started today.

As I stood outside the main office, my eyes wandered the hallways and watched the students laugh with each other and mess around before homeroom. I felt like an outsider, I saw a guy with their arm around a girl, I watched as a couple snuck in a quick kiss before heading off to class. I never had a relationship in my old high school. I went out on one date with a friend of mine but nothing came of it but I don't mind being by myself.

My thoughts slowly drifted away as I heard my name being called out. "Emily Stone" the voice came from behind the desk. I walked over to the desk where a lady gave me a list of my courses and a welcome package.

"If you run into any problems or have any questions, just stop by and I will be happy to help you out," the sweet older lady said handing me all my information, "I thought maybe you needed help to at least find your homeroom, so I asked my daughter to stop by, since you are in the same room."

"Thanks," I said quietly as I turned around to see this beautiful blonde waiting for me to finish up. I saw the guys stare at her as they passed by. I even heard a few catcalls, but it didn't even faze her, she completely ignored it.

"Hey Emily, I'm Samantha, but just call me Sam, that's what everyone does." She headed out of the office. "So, where are you from?" She asked as I quickly followed her.

"I just moved here from Houston," I said quietly.

"So, why did you move to Buffalo? I couldn't imagine moving to somewhere cold, we are all trying to move south after graduation," Sam laughed softly.

I wasn't sure if I wanted to share all my family issues on the first day. "Um, Family, I moved to be closer to my mom," I smiled.

"I hear ya, my parents are divorced too," she smirked as she stopped at the door and turned, "This is our homeroom."

I looked into the room and saw that most of the kids were already there and seated. They were all chatting to each other about summer vacation and looking through class schedules to see which classes they had together. At least some things don't change in a different school.

I walked into the room and Sam introduced me to the teacher. She pointed me to the empty desk and luckily Sam was sitting next to me. She must have read the look on my face as I looked around.

She chuckled, "It's ok, people are friendly here. You have your normal cliques but it's not too bad. I can introduce you to my friends. I've been friends with them since we were little kids, they will welcome you with open arms. What's your first class?"

I grabbed the sheet of paper sticking out of my folder, "Chemistry."

"I'm in that class also so just stick with me today, I will help you out."

My focus turned towards the door as he entered. He was gorgeous, dark brown hair, dark eyes and he appeared to be in great shape. He wore a button down shirt opened to reveal a white t-shirt underneath it. He was with a group of friends, laughing and talking; as he got closer I could smell his cologne and realized I hadn't stopped staring at him.

I heard Sam laugh softly, "His name is Eric." She was also watching him move to his seat. "You can stop staring I've seen him have one girlfriend in four years. He's into football and believe me that's it. I have flirted with the best of them and haven't gotten anywhere. I think every girl in our class wants to date him but everyone knows it's all about football and that's it."

I just couldn't take my eyes off of him, it wasn't like me. He had this look about him that was irresistible to me. I wasn't into "girl stuff" but noticed myself wondering if I looked ok. I was average looking and fit, or at least tried to be, my dark hair comes down past my shoulders, I wear it back to keep it out of my eyes. I have brown eyes and I wear contacts because I hate my glasses. My breathing stopped suddenly when his eyes met mine for the first time.

His stare was intense, like he was trying to figure out who I was and where I came from. I quickly turned away and looked at Sam for guidance.

She whispered, "That's the most I've seen him look at someone in years, unbelievable, you are here for ten minutes and already have the eyes of the most gorgeous guy in our class."

I glanced back to him but he was already back talking to his friends. My thoughts were interrupted when the first bell went off.

****

The day was going by fast, learning people's names and trying to figure out where to go was getting easier. Thank God for Sam though, she stuck by me on the first day, I felt like a puppy dog never leaving her side.

As we headed towards the lunchroom, I kept looking around, I don't know if I was looking at all the new faces or trying to find his face again. I haven't seen him since homeroom and was curious to find out more information about him. Though, if he was that big into football, that didn't bode well for me seeing how I can't play sports and barely can watch them. Sam kept talking to me but I couldn't really hear her, I just kept thinking about Eric.

The cafeteria was a lot bigger then what I was used to. I could tell that every class was represented here from the small freshman to the tall seniors. I wasn't into eating horrible cafeteria food so I told Sam I would see her back at the table and headed towards the salad bar.

I scanned the lunchroom over the sneeze guard, watching all the kids laughing and enjoying their time off from class. As I looked around, I caught out of the corner of my eye, Eric. He just entered the room with all his jock friends. They headed to a huge table in the back of the lunch room. I couldn't take my eyes off of him, he had so much confidence in his walk. He seemed to know that all the girls were watching him but he didn't focus on that. I didn't know how it was possible but it made him even sexier. He walked passed a table of freshman girls who all turned to stare at him. I laughed lightly as they couldn't turn away.

Distracting myself, I continued to pick out my vegetables, I quickly grabbed my tray, realizing too late that my bottle of water was about to fall to the floor. As I tried to make a quick move for it, it didn't end up on the floor but in someone's hand. As I looked up, I couldn't think of anything to say.

"Hi," Eric said.

I just stared at him, those eyes were just breathtaking and his voice was deep and so sexy. Speak Emily, "Hi."

He smiled as he placed my bottle back on the tray for me, "You're the new girl, right?"

"That's me," I said softly, trying not to focus on my shaky voice, "I'm Emily."

"Welcome to Buffalo, Emily. I heard you were from the South."
People were already talking about me, I'm not sure if that's good or bad, "Houston," I said quietly.

He nodded as his eyes never left mine, he looked as if he wanted to say something else but quickly decided against it, "Well, see you around." Before I could blink he was off with his friends in the line for some greasy, nasty food.

I got closer to my new lunch table as Sam quickly grabbed me and pulled me into the seat next to her. "What did he say to you? Spill!"

I just laughed at her, "It was nothing, he stopped my water from falling on the ground."

"I saw you talking to him, come on start gossiping."

I laughed, "He said people were already talking about me."

"Yeah, some of the football guys think you are hot and the stuck up cheerleaders don't like that too much. But, don't think twice about it."

I smiled as I looked around the table and tried to remember names and faces. Everyone has been so nice to me so far, my nerves were starting to relax. As I ate my salad, I listened to all the gossip.

Angie was the redheaded girl who kept discussing her summer trip to Spain. She had tons of pictures and wanted to share them with everyone.

Next to her was Mike, he was cute and very nice. But, I think Angie liked him, her hands were all over him. He kept nodding at her as she described in detail her trip.

Sam was busy discussing the upcoming Homecoming events with someone who just walked over to her with paperwork. I'm assuming she was on the committee, sounds like the school was big into supporting the football team.

My eye spotted Eric again as a huge roar of laughter came from his table. He looked gorgeous as he harassed his friends. I could stare at his smile all day long.

I didn't understand where this was all coming from I was never this big into guys. Maybe it was something about the northern guys. I watched as his group left the cafeteria.

"I have gym next, where do I go?" I asked grabbing my bag.

"Come on, Emily. I have gym too, I will show you to the locker room," Angie said as we got up from the table.

"Thanks." I waved goodbye to Sam and followed Angie.

I followed her out of the room and headed over to the gym. As I walked in, I was shocked how big it was. It was a full size gym with a full size pool off in another room. Angie opened the locker room door as we walked in. Another surprise, it was bright with tons of lockers, full showers, bathrooms.

"Unbelievable."

"What?" Angie asked

"We just didn't have anything like this in our old school."

Angie laughed, "Yeah, well, you go to a school now that takes their sports very seriously. They remodeled everything about 3 years ago, after we won the state championship in football."

I smiled at her, as the coach came into the room. She discussed what we were going to do this year, mapped out all the activities, discussed the dress code for gym and said it was a free period since it was the first day.

"Good, let's go sit on the bleachers," Angie said pulling me out of the room.

We climbed up a few rows and sat down. The guys were already out on the court, playing basketball to pass the time. I saw

Eric under the net, grabbing the ball and running back down towards me. He was so graceful, unlike me. He passed it to a teammate, who quickly passed it back to him, but in a blink of an eye, he passed it too wide and it headed straight for the bleachers. I didn't have time to move as it hit me right in the face.

My hands quickly went up to the nose as I heard Angie call for the coach to come over. They had an ice pack on me in no time. This was embarrassing, great way to start a new school.

"Angie, can you walk her down to the nurse's office? I want to make sure nothing is broken" the coach said as she helped me down the bleachers.

That's when I heard his voice, "I will take her, Coach Bennett, it's my fault," Eric said as he grabbed my arm.

"Thanks Eric."

We headed out of the gym and I followed him down the hall.

"I'm so sorry, Emily," He remembered my name. "I got distracted for a second and before I snapped out of it, your nose got in the way."

"It's ok. I should have told you that I'm prone to accidents." I laughed softly.

"I still feel bad. Are you going to be ok?" He looked into my eyes as he talked. I could have gotten lost in them.

"I will be fine. I don't think it's broke, just sore. Your friend has a hard throwing arm."

"Yeah, Todd is a big jock. He gets so into it, he probably didn't even realize that the girls had entered the gym." He laughed.

We entered the nurse's office and he sat next to me. "You don't have to stay; I know you probably want to get back to your game."

He smiled, "It's ok. I want to make sure you are ok first."

He just kept looking at me, like he wanted to say something, but at that point, the nurse walked in.

THE BARRIER

I walked into the house around four in the afternoon. My mom was still at work so I started cleaning out my backpack and doing my homework for the next day. I managed to get through day one with only a bruised nose. Not bad. I headed to my mom's bedroom upstairs to look around her makeup case, hoping I could cover up the dark bruises around my nose.

As I looked into the mirror, smearing the cover up around my nose, I noticed for the first time that I was attractive. It was the first time I ever thought about it or even noticed it. At some point, I grew up. I smiled at myself as I finished up.

I heard my mom's car pull into the driveway around five. I headed to the kitchen as I heard her come in the side door. I ran down the stairs and met her at the dining room table.

"Oh my God!" She dropped her purse onto the table and ran over to me.

"I guess the cover up, didn't work, huh? It's ok, Mom. I had an accident in gym class."

Laughing as she worked the cover up into the skin more, "Is it broke?"

"No, just bruised. It's ok. Just hurts a little."

"What a great way to start the first day of school, huh?" She smiled, "Well, whatever you want for dinner, you want to go out?"

"Sure, where do you want to go?"

"I will take you to place in town, great food."

She grabbed her purse again and we headed to a local restaurant. As we pulled in, I noticed a lot of kids from school were there, must be a popular hang out in town.

Mom walked in ahead of me as we were seated. I glanced around looking at faces, some people recognized my mother and said hello.

"So, tell me about your first day, Em."

"It was ok. Classes were good, found a couple of friends."

"Well, that's good to hear! I know it must be tough meeting new people."

"Yeah, but people were really nice to me today, so it helped."

As our food came, we continued to discuss classes and my nose incident.

As we were finishing up our meal, I saw Sam come in with her mom.

"Hey Emily!" She said running over to the table.

"Hey Sam," I smiled, "This is my mom."

"Hey," She smiled, "Can I talk to you before you go, Emily?"

I looked at my mom, "Go ahead, I will just go talk to Mrs. Howell over there."

I got up from the table and headed outside with Sam. The air had already cooled down for the evening. I'm not used to that, as I started to rub my arms up and down with my hands.

"What's up?" I asked walking down the sidewalk and stopping in front of my mom's car.

"How's the nose?"

I rubbed it softly. "It's ok. Hurts a little, but I will survive."

She smiled, "Well, rumor has it that Eric walked you down to the nurse's office."

I smirked at her, "Yeah, he did. It was sweet of him."

"Well, I heard from Angie that when he got back to the gym, he told Todd that he better watch his aim next time." She smiled at me.

I just sat there staring at her. My heart was beating faster now. I felt like I had butterflies in my stomach. This was not normal for me. "I'm sure he was just being macho in front of his friends, nothing more."

"You don't understand, he has had one girlfriend since we started high school. Every girl in our class has asked him out and has gotten nowhere, his father is very strict about that stuff. It's always been football, football, football. So, every girl in school is going to be talking about this, just a warning."

I laughed softly.

"Maybe someone has finally broken through the barrier."

I saw my mom leave the restaurant, "I gotta run, see you tomorrow in school."

When I got home, I went right into the bedroom and laid back on my bed grabbing a book to read. But, I couldn't focus. I kept thinking about what Sam had told me. Did I break through the barrier? Was she right? I started thinking about school the next day, thinking about the clothes I should wear, thinking about my hair. This isn't like me.

I sat there for a moment and I knew I had to have something that would impress Eric. I got up and started to dig through my closet, finding nothing but old faded clothes. I needed a shopping trip, maybe Angie or Sam would be up for one this weekend. I jumped when I heard my mom enter my room.

"What's going on, Em?"

"I'm just looking through my clothes trying to pick out something to wear tomorrow."

"We are going to have to go shopping soon for you. We need to start getting you ready for Buffalo's winter season," She laughed, "It's going to be a brand new experience for you."

"Lucky me, maybe we could go this weekend? I would like to pick up some new things."

"Sure, sounds like fun. So, I didn't mean to eavesdrop, but I couldn't help myself, I hear you may have eyes for a boy already."

"Mom."

"What? I love having you back in my life that means girl talk. Who is it?"

I just stared at her.

"Come on give me a name at least."

"Eric."

"Eric who?"

"I honestly don't know his last name yet, Mom. Sam was telling me about him, but it never came up. I just know every time he was around me, I can't think of words to say and my mind gets all jumbled up."

"That's so sweet, Honey. You have a crush. I can't wait to see this guy."

"Mom, Stop. Really, it's nothing."

"Oh really? Is that why you are digging through your closet, trying to find something to wear that will make you look nice, huh?"

I didn't say anything I just let her keep talking. She was having fun. As she left my room I could hear her softly laughing.

THE FOOTBALL GAME

The second day of school was easier. I knew where I was going at least. Sam ran up to me before third period and stopped me in the hallway.

"You look great today! I need to borrow those jeans," She giggled, "I wonder if you wore your most incredible pair of jeans to impress anyone special?"

Now I laughed, "You are too much. I'm just trying to remember where my classes are, that's all."

"Sure." Sam said leaving me behind with a smirk.

I headed up the stairs towards the art room. I was looking forward to this class, I love drawing. It came natural to me and it was relaxing. I always seemed to float into my drawing and become part of the sketch.

As I entered the room for the first time, it was huge, just like everything else in this school. Easels stood in the middle of the room, all the art supplies were neatly arranged around the room. Huge tables were mixed in and most of the students were already seated so I quickly found an empty table and sat down. I was looking around, when I saw Eric enter. I watched him as he said hello to a few people in the front of the room and headed towards me.

I quickly adjusted my t-shirt and made sure my hair was ok.

"Is this seat taken?" He asked.

"No."

He sat down next to me and grabbed his notebook.

"So, how's the nose?"

"It's ok. Still sore, but I will survive, great way to make a first impression, huh?" I laughed as I turned back to my notebook, waiting for class to start.

"I'm really sorry about that."

"It wasn't your fault, I would blame Todd first."

"True, ok, we will go with that," He laughed as he went back to his notebook.

"So are you into art?" He asked looking at me.

"Yeah, I love drawing. How about you?"

He laughed and shook his head, "No, just trying to fill in a credit with an easy class."

I laughed as the teacher arrived and started going through the syllabus. The class was perfect for me. I knew it would quickly become my favorite forty-five minutes of the day.

"First, I want to get a grasp on how creative you are. So, take your pads and pencils and start sketching. I will be around to help you out and give you some pointers, whatever you want to draw."

I grabbed my pencil and started drawing my favorite thing, scenery. I don't know what it is; I love the peace of it. The trees, the meadow, the flowers, just makes me want to jump into the picture and lay in the grass.

"That's great, Emily, let me show you a technique that will help you bring this more to life," Mrs. Claire said as she grabbed the pencil, "Just wonderful, keep up the good work, and Eric, that's, um, nice."

"I guess I need some work, huh?" He laughed as he stopped drawing, "It's ok; I'm more of the hit people in the nose kind of guy." I chuckled and smiled at him.

"You have a great smile." He said looking at me quickly and returning his gaze to his notepad.

"Thanks." I turned back to my pad, smiling.

"So, are you coming to the football game on Saturday?" He asked, trying to finish his really bad drawing of something.

"I don't know anything about it."

"Well, it's against our rival school it's also the first game of the season. Everyone in town comes out."

"Um, I guess I could. I was never really into sports but I guess that could change," I smiled at him, "What time?"

"Four."

I nodded at him as the bell rang. I started to grab my stuff as the pencil started to roll off the desk, I went to grab it as I felt his hand touch mine as he grabbed for it as well. He handed it back to me, "Thanks."

We both got up and headed out the door into the busy hallway, I lost him when his friends came running by and took him off into a different direction. I walked back to my locker and Angie was waiting for me.

"Hey, so how's it going today?"

"Good, I'm getting better at finding things," I smiled at her as I tried to remember my combination. I reached in to grab my calculus book and put away my art supplies.

"Have you seen Eric today?"

I smiled thinking back to art class, "Yeah, we were just in art class together."

"And?"

"Just did our drawings."

Angie smiled, "I just can't believe it, I'm so jealous."

"Hey, are you going to the football game on Saturday?" I asked as I closed my locker, looking back at her, out of the corner of my eye, I saw him at his locker he looked back at me and smiled. I think my heart stopped.

"Of course, are you going to come with us?"

"Yeah, I think I am," I said as I started to head towards math class.

****

The last bell rung as everyone ran to their lockers and out the door to catch their busses. Since I walk home, I waited for the crowds of people to leave the hallway before I started to gather all my books that I needed for my homework. Sam and Angie walked by as they were heading towards the main office, waiting for Sam's mother to give them a ride home.

"Hey Emily, I heard you are coming with us to the game on Saturday, I'm so excited!" Sam said leaning against the locker next to mine. A group of guys walked by staring at Sam and winking, "What's their problem?"

"Yeah Sam, it's so tough having every guy in school want you," Angie laughed as she sat on the floor, going through her book bag.

"Not every guy, Angie. I know one guy that I can't get," Sam laughed as she stared at me.

I didn't say anything, just laughed as I shut my locker, "Are you finished?"

"So, you want to meet us here on Saturday?" Angie asked as she stood up again, bushing off her jeans.

"Yeah, that's fine. Hey, you guys wouldn't be interested in doing some clothes shopping early Saturday, would you? I just realized that I have nothing in my closet that I like anymore. My mom was going to take me, but I would rather go with you guys."

Sam gasped, "I would love that, let's hit the mall around noon, we will get you some new outfits and I will borrow my mom's car and pick you up."

I smiled, "Sounds good to me." I stopped as we started to walk through the front door, "Oh crap, I forgot my government book I have an essay due tomorrow. I will see you guys tomorrow."

"See ya!" Angie yelled over her shoulder.

I headed back into school and turned to walk down the deserted hallways. It was weird after hours. There was no hustle, no loud laughing or talking. I got to my locker and grabbed my government book.

I turned to head back to the doors, when I saw Eric turn the corner he was wearing his football jersey and a pair of shorts. He stopped in front of me, "Hey you."

I smiled at him, "Nice uniform."

He smiled this time, I could get lost in his smile, "Practice, I forgot some of my stuff in my locker."

"Cool, well, I won't keep you then." I smiled at him again as I started to walk around him. I felt his hand grab my arm lightly. I turned back to him, looking into his eyes.

"I wanted to ask you something quickly," He said, moving slightly closer to me.

I couldn't speak I just stood there waiting to hear what he had to say to me.

"I was wondering if Saturday night, after the game, if you would like to grab a bite to eat with me. I would take you home, if you needed me to."

I couldn't believe it, he was asking me out. Of course I wanted to go, but the words were not leaving my mouth. I opened my lips but nothing came out.

"If you have plans already, it's ok; I just figured I would ask."

"No, no, no plans. I would love too." I smiled at him.

"Awesome," He grabbed my hand lightly with his.

Another football player came running down the hallway and yelled, "Mason, get outside, coach is getting ticked off with you."

He quickly dropped my hand, "Sorry, football practice." He ran to his locker and smiled at me as he passed me and ran back into the gym, the doors closed and he was gone. I just stood in the hallway; I can't believe I have a date for Saturday night with Eric. I needed to call Sam as soon as I got home. I headed out the back door of the school, looking over the football field.

I saw him line up with his teammates and throw the ball down the field. He looked so confident in his play. He was having fun; I saw it on his face when he took his helmet off. Just as I turned to walk down the stairs; I could swear I saw him look at me and smile.

I got home a little after four since I was taking my time, enjoying the sunshine. I went up into my bedroom and got all my homework done in record time. I needed to call Sam before I went downstairs to start dinner.

"Hello?"

"Hey Sam, it's Emily."

"Hey girl, what's up?"

"I have some interesting news for you."

"What? Tell me!"

"I have a date Saturday night."

"WHAT?"

"You heard me, I have a date."

"What happened, I want details," Sam screamed into the phone.

I started to go into details about my conversation with Eric. I was smiling the entire conversation, I was so happy and that's when I heard my mom's car pull up.

"Sam, I need to run, my mom is home and I forgot I'm in charge of dinner tonight."

"Ok, we will talk tomorrow, sweet dreams, Em."

I laughed as I hung up the phone, running over to the freezer and grabbing the lasagna, my mom walked in as I started up the oven.

"Hey Mom, dinner will be a little late, I was late getting home today."

She smiled, "It's ok. I will go hop into the shower first. Why are you smiling from ear to ear?"

"No reason."

"Does it have something to do with Eric somebody?"

"Mason."

She looked at me and smiled, "Nice family. I grew up with his mom, we were close friends throughout high school. We lost touch after I moved to Texas."

"Well, he asked me out Saturday night."

"Really? That's exciting!"

"So, I hope you don't mind, but Sam and Angie are going to take me shopping on Saturday afternoon, I know that we were supposed to go."

"That's fine, you will have more fun with your friends. Just remind me to give you some money before you leave."

"Thanks, Mom." I smiled as I hugged her, "I'm really glad I decided to move here."

I walked away to set the table as I thought I saw my mom shed a tear.

****

The first week of school flew by, I was so busy learning the layout of the school and finding my classes that I didn't realize the weekend had arrived. As I woke up in the morning, the sun was shining through the shades already. I looked over at my alarm clock and it read eight forty-five already. I stretched as I got out of bed. I ran my hand through my hair and moved quickly into my bathroom. I dreamt of him last night, which was first for me. I dreamt of what his lips would feel like on mine. I have kissed a guy before just not a lot of them. Throughout the week, we exchanged glances and talked more in art class but I was getting more and more excited about tonight's date.

I needed to find something fun to wear, I've never been to a football game plus I wanted to look good for him. I was hoping Sam would lead me in the right direction.

I stepped out of the shower and threw on my jeans and t-shirt and headed downstairs for breakfast.

"Good morning."

"Hey Sweetie, I left some money on the counter for you. I need to run to work for awhile. So, I will probably miss you later on. Have a great time tonight and I want details when you get home."

I smiled at her; she was a big kid at heart.

"Try to be home before midnight though, ok?" There was the mother side of her.

"No problem, Mom. I will give you a call at some point today." She smiled and kissed my cheek as she ran out to her car.

I finished up my housework and waited for Sam to arrive. I heard her car pull up around noon as she beeped the horn for me. I ran out the side door and saw that Angie was with her.

"Hey Em! I brought along some more help, figured we could make it a girlie day."

"Great, I need all the help I can get. I've never been to a football game before, I don't even know where to start."

"No problem, we have been talking about this and we are prepared," Angie said as she turned to talk to me, "I can't believe you have a date tonight. Where is he taking you?"

"I have no idea, we were cut off so he never really finished his thought," I said.

"You are going to have so much fun tonight."

I smiled as Sam pulled into a parking spot at the mall. We kept going in and out of stores, trying to get a feel of what I wanted to wear.

"Well, here's an idea," Sam grabbed a pair of jean shorts off the rack and handed them to me, "Go try these on."

"Sam, these are the tiniest things I've ever seen."

"Yeah, but they will look awesome on you, go!"

I grabbed the shorts and headed to the dressing room. I slid off my jeans and pulled the shorts on as they barely covered my butt. I couldn't help but laugh.

"What's so funny in there?" Sam asked.

"Sam, these are crazy, my mother will kill me if she saw me wear these."

"Oh stop it, let me see them."

I walked out of the dressing room and twirled for her. "Well?" Both girls just stood there.

"Why are you hiding those legs, are you kidding me? You are buying those. He will go crazy the minute he sees you."

I laughed as I turned to go back into the dressing room, catching out of the corner of my eye the guys in the store were all staring at me. I started to blush and grabbed for my jeans.

"Ok, now that we have the bottom, we need a top," Sam said, like she was on a mission.

Angie gasped, "I got it! She needs a jersey."

"Angie, we are not going to cover up her legs, we just found them!"

"No, we will get her a girl one! They have pink jerseys."

"Pink? I don't think I should wear pink," I said with a strange look on my face.

"No, it will be perfect, let's go." Angie said dragging me into another store.

She managed to find a pink football jersey. It wasn't that bad either. I looked in the mirror and thought that the girls really did a good job.

As we left the mall, I realized it was three already. I had Sam drop me off at home so I could change and meet them at school.

I stood in my room, taking the tags off my new clothes. I was nervous but excited at the same time. I had a date with the quarterback of the football team.

I grabbed my new shorts and jersey and put them on. Not too bad, Emily. I grabbed my hair and threw it up into a ponytail and reached for my sneakers. Once I was done, I looked into the mirror and smiled. I do have nice legs.

I ran downstairs so I could leave before my mom got home, I didn't need to hear about the shorts as the phone started to ring,

"Hello?"

"Emily, it's your Dad."

"Hey Dad, how's it going?"

"Not too bad, miss you."

"Miss you too, Dad."

"Getting used to the different weather?"

"It's not too bad yet. Today is really warm, so it's good."

"Good to hear, how's your mom?"

"She's good, she's at work right now and I really need to leave myself, I'm going to the school's football game."

"Football, really?"

"Yeah, shocking, right?"

"Well, I won't keep you then. I just wanted to hear your voice. Say hello to your mom for me and call me when you get a chance."

"Ok Dad, is everything ok?" I said hearing something in his voice.

"Yeah, I just wanted to call with some news."

"What's that?"

"Well, you are going to have another sibling."

I just stared at the wall. I didn't say a word and I think I forgot to breath.

"Em?"

"Yeah, I'm here."

"Isn't that great news, Beth is four months pregnant."

"Wow, Dad. I'm speechless. I mean, I thought you were done with that part of your life."

"Well, you know that Beth always wanted kids. I know I'm much older than she is, but she wanted to experience it, who was I to deny her of that?" She does get whatever she wants after all.

"Dad, I really need to go. I will talk to you later. Congrats." I said, as I hung up the phone. I couldn't believe my ears. He was fifty-eight years old. Are you kidding me? I didn't even realize he could still do that! I just shook my head, trying to get those thoughts out of it.

I walked slowly to school. How could one conversation knock the wind out of your sails so quickly? I can't let it bother me. I have been waiting for this minute all day long. I will just have to deal with my sexually charged father later.

As I walked around to the back of school, the stands were pretty full and the teams were already on the field. I scanned the bleachers for Sam and Angie. I turned again to look at the field. I saw Eric walking down the sidelines toward me. I walked over to the fence that separated us.

"Hey Emily," He said as he leaned on the fence.

"Hey Eric."

"I'm so happy you are here and you look fantastic."

I blushed slightly, "Thanks."

"EMILY!"

I turned to see Angie waving at me from the top of stands. I waved back slightly, not wanting to look ridiculous in front of Eric.

"I think Angie and Sam are waiting for you," He said, "I will meet you at the back of the gym doors after the game, ok?"

"Sure, I can't wait," I smiled at him again and headed towards the bleachers. I could feel his eyes on me as I started to climb up towards my friends. I could also feel the eyes of every guy watching me. I blushed again.

Sam grabbed me when I got to the top, "Oh my God, you look hot!"

I laughed at her.

"You should have seen him watch you walk up those stairs I thought his eyes were going to pop out."

"Come on."

"Angie, tell her!"

"He was, Em. It was unbelievable."

I laughed again as I heard the whistle start the football game.

We would stand up and cheer with the crowd. I tried to follow the game without a lot of luck. I just followed what everyone else was doing. At half time, I watched the cheerleaders do their thing. They definitely got the crowd into the game. At the end of the cheer, they came off the field as I watched the one girl go up to Eric and throw her arms around him.

"And who is that?" I asked.

Angie laughed, "Jealous already, huh?" I shot her a look. "That would be Janice. His only girlfriend that I know of, she is a total bitch. They broke up last year after Eric chose football over her."

I felt stupid watching them, we haven't even been on a date yet, how could I be jealous of her? She was gorgeous, just like Sam, long blonde hair, perfect legs and of course, a perfect top. I look down at myself and realized I wasn't built like that. I wasn't small by any means but I definitely wasn't a "D" cup like her.

"Emily, don't worry about it, they broke up. He's going on a date with you tonight not her," Angie said bringing me back to life.

We watched the rest of the game and Eric was amazing. He definitely has a career in football ahead of him. We ended up winning the game.

As the bleachers emptied, I watched the team go into the locker room. I walked down the stairs with Angie and Sam and stopped at the bottom.

"Have an awesome time tonight and call me tomorrow, I want details," Sam said hugging me.

I hugged them both good bye and turned to walk over to the gym doors hopping up onto the low concrete wall and sat waiting for Eric to come out. I watched some of the cheerleaders huddled around the back doors waiting for the boys. I moved slightly, so they couldn't see me waiting there.

"Did you see her? I can't believe he would be interested in her? She doesn't fit in here," I heard as Janice came around the corner with two other cheerleaders that I didn't know, "He will always be mine."

I just sat there in the shadows, not wanting to hear this. I started to smile because I knew I could win this battle. He wanted to date me not her. I'm not a mean person, but part of me thought this could be fun.

I saw him come through the doors, dressed in his jersey and jeans. He looked around and I knew he was looking for me. My eyes caught his and I waved at him. His face lit up as he pushed right by Janice and headed over to me.

"Hey you," He said, "What did you think of your first football game?"

"You were amazing, I never realized how much fun a game could be," I smiled at him, watching over his shoulder as Janice watched us. I hopped off the wall, "So, where are we going?"

"It's up to you, did you want to hit the popular hangout or did you want something quieter."

I thought about it for a minute, "Quiet."

He smiled at me, "You got it." He grabbed my hand and led me right past where Janice and her cheerleaders were standing. If looks could kill, I would be dead by now.

He walked me across the school parking lot and opened the door of his Mustang for me.

"Nice car."

"Thanks, it was an early birthday gift from my dad."

"Wow, I got clothes for my birthday," I laughed as he shut the door for me. I watched him as he walked around the car and got in.

He started up his car and sped out of the parking lot. I was a little tense at first, not used to him or his driving style, but once he was past the school, he slowed down a little more. I turned to look at him and he was looking at me, smiling.

"So, you like football, I take it?" I asked him.

"I love it. There is something about the feel of the field underneath you. The guys are always looking after my back, it's just fun. I'm getting a full scholarship to Syracuse next year."

"Wow, that's incredible! I haven't picked a school yet. I have all the applications sitting at home but no motivation to do anything yet."

"Yeah, it's scary," He said as he pulled into a small restaurant parking lot, "Here we are, they have the best burgers in town and no one knows about it."

He came around and opened the door for me again, I swung my legs out the door and he reached for my hand, "Thanks," I said smiling at him.

He started to walk me down the sidewalk, when he stopped and turned towards me, "Have I mentioned how incredible you look tonight?"

I blushed again, "Yeah, you said something earlier."

"Just wanted to make sure, because you really do. Too bad you can't wear those shorts to school."

"Why couldn't I wear them?"

He smirked at me, "Because I would be punching every guy who looks at you."

I blushed again.

He opened the door for me as we walked inside. It was very quiet. There were only about five other people inside. They all looked when we walked in.

He leaned over and whispered in my ear, "See, just like that, if that old man doesn't stop staring at you, I may lose it right here."

I laughed a little bit too loudly; he dropped my hand as he walked over to a table and pulled the chair out for me. I smiled as I sat down. He came and sat down right next to me.

He ordered the double bacon cheeseburger with fries. He laughed, "I'm hungry after I play."

I ordered the regular hamburger. I'm not much of a meat eater, but I didn't want to look silly eating a salad at a burger joint.

"So, tell me about yourself," He asked me as he grabbed my hand again.

"Well, I'm from Texas, I moved here to be closer to my mom. She's from here, she actually went to school with your mom."

"I heard that, when I mentioned to my mom about tonight, she said that she was going to call your mom to catch up."

I smiled again, "Um, I really into reading, writing, drawing, stuff like that."

"That's cool. You are really good at it, I saw your drawing in class the other day. You have talent."
"Thanks."

He stroked my fingers with his.

"I have a question for you," I said looking at him.

"Shoot."

"Rumor is, you have only dated Janice since you started high school."

He started to laugh, "That's not a question."

"The question is, why me? If you aren't really into dating, why pick me? I've heard that every girl in school has asked you out, I only started here five days ago." He smiled at me and looked into my eyes, "You caught my eye. You are different than the girls here, you weren't all over me, and you were quiet. You seemed really nice and…"

"And?"

"And…your eyes did me in. I can't stop looking at them."

I blushed again, he had that effect on me.

"And that look you get when I say something nice to you, it's like you don't believe me or something, it's such a turn on for me."

I looked down at the table, "Well, I think someone already wants my head on a platter."

"Who?" He asked seriously.

"Janice."

He laughed, "Yeah, I could see that. Don't worry about her. She's all bark. I have no interest in her anymore that ended a year ago."

"Can I ask why?"

He looked at me and smiled, "She was a lot to handle. I couldn't make her happy and continue to play football. My father is very strict about football and thought Janice was taking up too much of my time."

I nodded, "So, I take it your Dad won't like me then?"

He smirked, "You planning on monopolizing all my time?"

I chuckled, "Maybe, we will have to see," I winked at him. I smiled again as the waitress sat our plates on the table.

The entire meal we ate and talked. Learning more about each other, I turned to look out the window and almost choked on my food.

"Eric?"

"Yeah?"

"Janice and her clone cheerleader friends just pulled in."

Eric moved to see around me and laughed, "Of course."

I giggled a little and watched him move closer to me, "You ready to leave?"

"Yes, please."

He smiled as he paid the bill and reached for my hand, "Come on."

We walked right past them, "Ladies."

"Hey Eric," Janice said stopping him with her arm, "Where are you going so fast, thought we could hang out."

"Not tonight, Janice, I'm busy," He said walking away from the group. As we approached the car, he laughed softly, "Man, she's going to be pissed off now." He opened the door for me again as I got in. My eyes caught Janice's and I swear I saw fire shooting out of them.

****
**

"Thanks for dinner, Eric," I said as he pulled into my driveway. I saw my mom's car in the driveway, "Damn." I said softly under my breath.

"What's wrong?" He asked concerned.

"Well, first, I forgot to bring a change of clothes, I don't think my mom will approve of these shorts,"

He laughed, "Does it help if I say I approve of them?"

I looked at him, "Then I forgot about a phone call I got earlier today from my dad, I just have to talk to my mom."

"You ok?"

"Just some family stuff I really don't want to deal with yet."

"Well, I have an idea. Why don't you wear my jersey inside, it will come down to your knees, your mom will think you have regular shorts on and not question you about it."

"Not bad!" I laughed.

He reached to take off his shirt, as he pulled it up, his t-shirt came up with it, before he could grab it, I will able to get a peek at his abs. I held my breath in. He was definitely in shape.

"Here, put this on." He handed me his jersey, I slid it on over my jersey and he was right, it was definitely longer, "Thanks Eric, you saved my evening."

He smiled at me, "Anytime."

"I will return it on Monday when I see you."

"No problem."

"Well, thanks again," I said as I started to get out of the car.

"Emily?"

"Yeah?" I said as I turned back to him.

He leaned closer to me, as his lips covered mine for the first time. I let a soft sigh come from my lips. He responded as his lips parted, I felt his tongue move over my lower lip, as I started to get lost in the kiss. His hand moved up into my hair as I pressed my hand gently to his chest. He slowly pulled away.

"Wow."

I was speechless, I looked up into his eyes.

"See you on Monday," I said as I got out of the car.

BREAKFAST

Sunday morning was uneventful. Mom was sleeping on the couch when I came into the house last night, so I was able to sneak past her and change my clothes. I put his football jersey on the back of my desk chair and stared at it all night long and fell asleep dreaming of our kiss.

I was helping my mom make Sunday breakfast and waiting for my grandparents to stop by but I couldn't stop thinking about Eric.

"So, since I was asleep last night, how was the date?"

"It was really nice, Eric was a perfect gentleman, opening doors, paying for dinner. It was a lot of fun."
She smiled at me as she flipped the bacon, "I'm so happy to hear that."

"There was something I needed to discuss with you though, yesterday before I left, Dad called." She didn't say anything. "He wanted to say hi and make sure I was adjusting ok."

"That was nice of him."

I could already tell the bitterness in her voice. He hurt her a lot when he cheated on her with Beth. Apparently, she was too old for him and he needed a younger model, as she puts it every time she tells the story.

"Well, he also had some other news."

"Like?"

"I don't know how to say this," I said watching her put down the spatula.

"Just say it."

"Beth is pregnant."

She quickly leaned against the kitchen counter.

"Mom, are you ok?"

She just stared at me, "Are you serious?"

"Unfortunately, yes."

"I can't believe it, do you know how long I fought with him wanting to give you a baby brother or sister and it was always out of the question, she comes in and he changes his mind."

"Honestly, Mom. I don't think it was his mind changing as much as it was Beth batting her eyelashes and getting what she wants."

The door bell rang.

"Don't mention this to your grandparents, you know how they get, ok?"

"Sure, Mom," I said as I ran to the front door to let my grandparents in.

"Hi Emily," My grandfather said giving me one of his big bear hugs.

"Hi Grandpa," I said, "Hi Grandma."

"Hi Sweetie, where's your mom?"

"She's cooking," I said as I went to close the front door, I peeked outside and saw Eric on his bike and the end of the driveway. I smiled, "I will be right back, ok?" I said as I shut the door behind me.

Eric rode his bike over to the front porch.

"Hey, Emily," He hopped off his bike and walked over to me.

"I can't stay out here very long my grandparents are over for breakfast."

"I'm sorry, I should have called first, but I couldn't stop thinking about you."

I blushed again, realizing that I look like crap. I was still in my pajama bottoms. My hands went up into the hair as I quickly ran my fingers through it. He must have been reading my thoughts.

"You look great."

I smiled at him. "Did you want me to run in and get your jersey?"

"No, you can keep it for now, it's an extra one. Actually, if you wanted to wear it next Friday at school, you could be my good luck charm," he said as he put his arm around my waist.

I smiled back at him as I heard the front door open. I jumped back a step.

"Emily, breakfast is ready," my mom said as she stepped out on the porch.

"Mom, this is Eric."

"Hi Eric, it's nice to meet you, I'm sorry to cut this short on you guys."

"Sorry for bugging you on Sunday, Mrs. Stone, I just wanted to stop by and say hi to Emily."

"No need to be sorry, have you eaten breakfast yet, Eric?"

"Not yet, no."

"Well, come on in. Any friend of Emily's is a friend of the family."

I looked at mom, she was just so wonderful. I mouthed thank you to her as Eric leaned his bike up against the house.

"Let me call your mom and tell her you are here, I would love to speak with her again."

After all the introductions, I took Eric's hand and pulled him into the dining room, I heard my mom finishing up with his mom.

"That's great, Alice, I can't wait to see you again! It's been way too long."

She hung up the phone, "Ok, Eric, you are all set. Have a seat and enjoy."

****

After breakfast, my mom and grandparents went into the living room to talk. I sat at the dining room table with Eric.

"Thanks for breakfast," He said.

"Sure, I'm glad my mom invited you."

He leaned over and whispered in my ear, "I miss the shorts."

I blushed again.

"There it is."

I laughed softly.

"Now, I told my mom you were the perfect gentleman last night, should I change my opinion?" I looked into his eyes.

"If only you knew what I was thinking," He smirked, "Your opinion would have changed fast."

I laughed again.

"Want to go outside?"

"Sure," he said, getting up from the table.

We headed out the side door to bypass all the adults. We started to walk across the lawn and into the open garage.

I sat on the stool and watched him look around. He came back over to me, standing in front of me.

"So, did you think about me last night?" I asked him.

"Yes, all night long."

I blushed again, looking up into his eyes, "Me too."

"You really don't know how beautiful you are, do you?"

I didn't say anything, I couldn't think of the right words.

"When you showed up at the game yesterday, with that outfit on, I thought I was crazy for asking you out. You were clearly out of my league."

I laughed, "Out of your league, are you serious?"

"Yeah, you looked so hot."

I smirked at him, "Well, I'm not going to argue with you."

He smirked at me, "See, and that only makes you sexier."

I had to remember that my grandparents were just in the house. I had to behave myself, "Well, there is one thing you haven't done yet and I'm wondering if it's because I'm not looking as hot today."

He smirked down at me again, "You would look hot in a garbage bag, Emily. But I think I know what you are referring to."

He leaned down to me as his lips gently touched mine. It was so gentle at first; it barely felt like he was there. Then I sighed again as he pulled away, "You have got to stop doing that or you will drive me crazy."

"I'm sorry, I promise to behave myself."

He leaned down again with a little more pressure, touching his lips to mine.

I heard the front door open and hopped off the stool quickly.

I heard him chuckle as I came out of the garage with Eric close behind.

"You guys leaving already?" I asked my grandparents as they got to the car.

"Yes, thanks for breakfast, it's always wonderful to see you," my Grandmother said as she kissed my cheek, "And Eric, a pleasure to meet such a nice boy."

"The pleasure is all mine," Eric said shaking my Grandfather's hand.

We watched as they pulled out of the driveway. I walked Eric over to his bike, "So, did you finish your English essay for tomorrow yet?" I asked him.

"Almost, I started it but my mind was distracted."

I laughed, "Oh yeah?"

"Yeah, but I will try my best when I get home."

I smiled, "Well, I will see you tomorrow."

"Ok, call me later if you get a chance."

"Sounds good to me."

Eric smiled as he got on his bike, leaning over slightly and kissing my cheek.

"Talk to you later, Emily."

"Bye."

When I got back inside the house, my mom was sitting on the couch with a huge smile on her face.

"What's on your mind, Mom?"

"I can see why you have a crush on him, he's adorable."

"Thanks, Mom. Are you ok?"

"Yes, Honey. I'm not going to lie. It hurts, but I can't let that man ruin my life again. I'm over it."

"Good for you, Mom, I'm proud of you."

"I'm just in shock over it. I just hope he doesn't forget his responsibilities to you."

I leaned against the doorway and looked at her, "Don't worry about me, Mom. I won't let him hurt either of us."

She smiled and made a spot for me next to her on the couch. "How do you think I feel? I will be eighteen years older than my little step-brother or step-sister."

She chuckled softly, "Well, you always wanted a brother or sister."

"Yeah maybe ten years ago."

"Well, you will be a great big sister."

I smiled at her, "So, you like Eric, huh?"

"Yes, he's very nice. I completely understand your interest in him. But Honey, just take it slow, ok? You are only eighteen, there are plenty of guys out there."

"Mom, stop."

"I'm not telling you not to enjoy it now I just don't want you to go overboard. I saw the way you looked at him. This is your first boyfriend. You never forget the first one."

It sounded strange, Eric is my boyfriend. I'm not even sure that's the case, we never talked about it, it was only one date. "Mom, it was one date, I don't even know what's going on yet."

She laughed, like she knew something I didn't.

"I'm going to go study." The day ended as quickly as it came, my one bright spot, tomorrow I would see him again.

IT'S OFFICIAL

Monday mornings are always difficult. You just finish the weekend and it feels like a lifetime until it comes around again. But, today was different, I knew the sooner I got going, the better my day would be.

I grabbed my jeans and my cute red t-shirt, as I looked into the mirror I noticed for the first time it hugged all the right spots. I still can't believe the way I was looking at myself. I used to grab whatever wasn't dirty and be content with that. But, I had a reason to look good. I clipped my hair back, leaving some of it over my shoulders. As I looked in the mirror one last time, I heard a car horn in the driveway.

I didn't know who it could possibly be this early in the morning. I walked over to the window and smiled, it was Eric.

"Emily, I think you have a ride to school!" My mom called up from downstairs.

I grabbed my school work and headed downstairs with my stuff.

"Wow, Emily. You look fantastic."

"Thanks, Mom, but really I'm not trying."

She laughed again, "Sure."

I hugged her good bye and headed out the door. I smiled at Eric as he got out of the car, "Emily, you look beautiful."

He opened the door for me and I slid into his awesome Mustang, "Thanks for the ride this morning, you really didn't need to do this. I don't mind walking."

He smiled, "How would it look if I let my girlfriend walk to school while I drove?"

I blushed again, "Girlfriend?"

This time he blushed a little, "I guess I never officially asked you, it's just I had such a great time Saturday night."

"I couldn't agree more with you."

He smiled, "So, would you be my girlfriend?"

"You sure your dad will be ok with this? I honestly don't want you to lose focus on football and cause you any trouble."

"Emily, you don't have to worry about that. I will handle my father."

I smiled at him as he pulled into his spot at the high school, "Let's see if this will answer it for you then."

I leaned over to him as I gently pressed my lips to his again. He responded very quickly to my lips, tasting them. I sighed again, knowing how much it drove him crazy. His hand quickly moved into my hair, crushed my lips more. I felt them part as his tongue moved with mine.

I suddenly realized we weren't alone anymore when I heard whistles coming from outside of the car. He pulled away, not paying any attention to them.

I smirked at him, "Did that answer your question?"

"Without a doubt."

I smiled at him, as we got out of the car and walked into school together, I knew Sam and Angie were waiting to attack me at my locker, I sensed it as I turned the corner and then, sure enough, I saw them there.

Eric laughed, "I'm sure your friends will be asking a million questions today."

I smiled at him, "I'm prepared, don't worry."

He walked me to my locker, "Hi Sam, Angie."

"Hey Eric, how was the weekend?"

He smiled at me, "The best of my life." He leaned down and kissed my cheek, "I will see you later on."

I opened my locker, knowing that four eyes were on me, waiting for something. I grabbed my first period stuff and shut the locker, heading towards home room.

"Emily Stone, I'm going to hurt you if you don't stop right now," Sam said grabbing my arm.

I laughed at her, "What's up, Sam?"

She just looked at me, "Are you kidding me? I'm so mad that you didn't call me Sunday and then I hear whispers that you are making out with him in his car this morning. I thought we were friends."

I hugged her, "We are, come on, sit next to me in home room."

I walked into the room, seeing Eric already sitting in his chair. He smiled and winked at me as I passed him. I sat next to Sam, starting to run through all the events of the weekend, every detail. I forgot what it felt like to have a close friend in my life.

"I can't believe he's your boyfriend, a week into school and you are dating the most handsome guy at this school, you are so lucky."

I smiled as I looked over at him, "Yeah, I am."

The day moved along quickly, I caught glimpses of Eric throughout the day but never had the chance to speak with him because his friends were busy distracting him and I wasn't the type to interrupt. I stopped at my locker before heading to lunch to meet up with Sam.

"Hi Emily," a voice said behind me as I turned around and shut my locker.

"Hi. Janice, right?" I asked.

"Yeah, I never had a chance to say hello and welcome you to our school last week."

"No problem and thanks."

"I just wanted to say that I think it's just fantastic that you are getting along with everyone here, everyone is talking about you and everyone thinks you are so great."

I just stared at her, no idea where this conversation was going, "Well, I'm just being me, I guess."

"Well, I wanted to talk with you for a second I know you are interested in Eric, who wouldn't be, right?" Janice laughed as she turned to look at her friends.

"Yeah, I guess I am."

"Well, you should know that we have some history between us. We have this on again off again relationship. It's very complicated, so I didn't want you to get confused and think he was available when he clearly isn't."

I just stared at her, my mind was laughing at her. I knew her type she thinks she was better than everyone, she got everything she wanted because she was drop dead gorgeous; I just left a situation like this behind in Texas when I moved away from my father and evil step mother. I wasn't ready to start another one here.

"Janice, I'm not sure what planet you are living on, but as of this morning, I'm dating Eric. I'm sorry you think differently," I said not believing that I just stood up for myself.

She didn't say anything as I walked away from her and her group of clones. I walked into the lunch room so upset. I tossed my books onto the table and sat down next to Angie.

"Em? What's wrong?" Angie asked very concern. Everyone at the table stopped talking and looked at me.

"I don't understand how people can be so rude to other people. Just because you are pretty doesn't give you the right to make other people feel like crap."

Sam got up from the other side of the table and moved to the seat next to me, "What happened?"

"Janice and I just had a conversation in the hallway." I said looking at the door as Eric and his football jocks came walking in.

He looked over at me and his smile quickly faded, he must have read my mind. I saw him leave his group and head in my direction.

Sam got up from her chair and moved back to her original position, leaving the chair empty for Eric.

"What's wrong, Emily?" He said sitting next to me.

"It's nothing," I said putting my head down into the arms.

"Sam? Tell me."

"Janice just confronted her in the hallway," She said looking at him, "Apparently, Janice is under the assumption that Emily is not allowed to date you."

Eric just stared at her, "Are you serious? Emily, is this true?"

I lifted my head, not realizing it had hit me so hard I had tears in my eyes, "Yeah, something like that."

Eric moved his hand across my cheek and wiped away the tears, "I told you on Saturday night, her bark is worse than her bite. But, I'm going to take care of this. I'm so sorry that this happened to you." He got up from his chair and left the cafeteria.

I stared at my friends, "I think it's just too much right now. After that phone call from my Dad, then having her say those things to me, it just reminded me of why I left Texas. I thought I had left all that crap behind me. But, apparently women are like that everywhere."

Angie put her arm around me, "Smile, Emily. It's ok, he's your boyfriend now! There are going to be a lot of jealous girls around here, but you know what, it doesn't matter, he likes you."

I smiled at her and Sam as she sat nodding and eating her lunch, "We love you, Emily and we are the only people who count!"

I laughed as I wiped my face. They were right and he was mine.

I left the lunchroom and headed to my least favorite class, gym. My nose started to hurt just thinking about it. I laughed softly as Angie and I entered the girls' locker room. We changed into our shorts and t-shirts and headed back into the gym.

I scanned the gym looking for Eric, of course, he was already playing basketball with his friends. He looked natural in his element, the way his body moved as he played basketball with his friends.

I heard Angie laugh next to me, "Just watch out for flying basketballs, ok?"

"No problem, I'm still recovering."

We went over to the Coach as she was discussing teams for our basketball drills. I hated this class, I had no clue when it came to sports and coordination. Luckily, she teamed me up with Angie. We passed the ball back and forth and talked the entire time.

"What do you think her problem is? I mean, she realizes that she can have any other guy in our class, right?" I asked her.

"True. But, she has always wanted Eric, it goes back before high school even. A bunch of us grew up on the same street together and she was always trying to impress him. I think it's like a conquest for her," She smiled tossing the ball back at me.

I smiled, "Yeah, I know, but where do you get off talking to someone like that? She doesn't know me from Eve."

"But you are messing with her man now, Em."

I laughed, "My man."

Angie laughed, "God, is this class over yet?"

I laughed as the coach blew the whistle, "Thank God." She said grabbing my arm, as I looked down the court and saw Eric, he winked at me again as he went into his locker room.

****

The week went by fast. Eric was picking me up every day in the morning and driving me home when he didn't have practice. If he missed me in the evening, I would get a phone call before my nine o'clock phone cut off, just to say good night to me. Janice kept her distance the rest of the week, I still wondered if he had words with her. He never mentioned it to me.

Friday morning was beautiful, I felt the sun coming through the window as I woke up; quickly jumped in the shower and grabbed his football jersey to wear on game day. I wore a simple white tank top underneath it and stuffed some of it into my jeans so I didn't hang past my knees. As I reached for my sneakers, I heard Eric pull into the driveway.

"Emily, Eric is here," my mom called from downstairs.

"Coming!"

I grabbed my books and headed downstairs.

"Nice jersey! I didn't know you played football."

"Funny Mom, he said it would bring him good luck, so who am I to argue." I said, kissing her cheek, "Don't forget, I'm staying at school for the game tonight, I will be home afterwards."

"Have fun!"

Eric was leaning against his car waiting for me when I walked out the side door.

"Hey Gorgeous," He said taking me into his arms, "That jersey looks amazing on you."

I laughed, "Oh yeah?"

We were starting to learn each others facial expressions and body movements. He started to lean down to kiss me, "Wait, I'm ninety-nine percent sure that my mom is staring out the window."

He peeked around my shoulder, "Yep, come on." He walked me around to the passenger side, opened the door for me and we headed to school.

Once we were in the parking lot, he shut off the car and leaned over again, our lips touched softly at first. He was a great kisser, but I didn't want to know how many girls he practiced on. My hand ran up the side of his face and lightly traced his cheekbone as I heard him sigh this time. His hand moved into my hair as he deepened the kiss, feeling his tongue move with mine. It was my turn to moan. I was surprised though by the sound of it. I have never made a noise like that before. He noticed it also as he quickly broke the kiss. His eyes met mine.

"I'm sorry, I don't know where that came from," I said, moving back into my seat.

"Don't be sorry," He reached for my hand, "It's just, I'm trying to remain a gentleman here but if I hear that sound again, I'm not sure if I can be. I don't want to ruin this by rushing anything."

"I know, I completely agree, it's just when I feel your lips on mine, I just lose it for that moment."

"I know the feeling, Emily," He said jumping out of the car and opening the door for me.

****

School was over quickly. Thank God. All I wanted to do was to see Eric again and Friday classes barely gave me the opportunity, plus being game day, he disappeared right after the last bell to start gearing up for the game.

I walked back to my locker and put all my stuff in it. I heard Janice walk behind me with her friends, "Nice jersey."

I controlled myself as my hand tightened around the strip of my book bag. I wanted so badly to say, "Isn't it," but I controlled myself and bit my tongue.

I leaned back against my closed locker waiting for Sam and Angie to show up, as I heard Sam's laughter come around the corner.

"Hey guys, what's so funny?" I asked.

"Janice is telling everyone that she wants to rip that jersey right off your back," She laughed, "It's so ridiculous. She's crazy."

I just looked at the floor, I was so mad that I knew I was going to say something horrible if I opened my mouth.

"It's ok, Emily, don't worry about it, how many times has Eric said he doesn't like her."

"I know."

"So, don't worry about it," She reached over and gave me a big hug, "Angie and I will beat her up if she comes anywhere near you."

I laughed softly.

"That's better," Angie said as she hugged me next, "I have a question though."

"What's that?" I asked her.

"What's it like to kiss him?"

"Get a grip, Angie, that's her boyfriend," Sam laughed.

I blushed at the question thinking back to this morning in his car, "It's amazing, awesome, wonderful all rolled into one."

Sam smiled at me, "I'm so happy for you, I guess this means you have a date to Homecoming, huh? And may I add a shot at Homecoming Queen, considering you are dating the quarterback," She laughed.

"I didn't even think about it, oh my God. First, I can't dance. Second, I've never gotten all dressed up before. Third, he hasn't asked me yet."

Angie smirked, "You are kidding right? I think it's implied at this point. You guys are dating."

Sam quickly jumped in, "I foresee another girl's day at the mall. We will all need dresses."

"Wait, did I miss something? Who are you guys going with?"

Sam pouted, "No one yet, but I have plans. I'm just sorting out of my options."

I smiled at her, "And you?"

Angie grinned, "Mike just asked me about an hour ago."

Sam and I both hugged her, "That's great, Angie!"

"So, when is it anyways?" I asked, being totally clueless about this stuff.

"Two weeks from Saturday night," Sam said.

"Ok, well, as soon as you figure out what lucky guy is taking you, we will go dress shopping," I said laughing at her, "Come on, let's go outside."

We walked out the back doors heading towards the field. The stands were already filling in with fans from both schools. We walked towards the fence and I saw Eric talking to the coach on the field, it looked like he was being yelled at, but I didn't know for sure. I also saw Janice practicing with her squad as I quickly turned and headed up the bleachers to catch up with Sam and Angie.

The game was fun but we ended up losing 37-17. Eric looked so mad after the game, he tossed his helmet against the fence and walked into the locker room. I looked at my friends for advice.

"It happens, you can't win them all. I'm sure he will be ok when he sees you."

"Yeah, go down and wait for him," Angie said standing up, "We will talk to you this weekend."

I nodded and walked down the bleachers, sat on my concrete wall and waited for him to come out of the locker room. No cheerleaders were around this time, they probably knew to leave him alone.

He came out about twenty minutes later and definitely had a different look on his face as he walked over to me and sat next to me.

"You ok?" I asked him as I put my hand on his back.

"You can't win them all right? That team was unbelievable. It was a challenge to get the ball down the field tonight."

"You looked good," I said biting my lip, not sure what I was going to say to him.

"Not really, but thanks anyways," He said smiling at me.

"Did you want me to walk home tonight? If you aren't in the mood for company that is fine, it's only a few blocks."

"No, I'm not letting you walk home at night, are you crazy? Come on." He said as he grabbed my hand and we headed to his car.

He opened the door for me and walked around to get into the drivers side. He didn't start the car right away, he just sat there.

"Are you sure you are ok?" I asked him, reaching for his hand.

He smiled again at me, "Yeah, I am now." He leaned over to me and kissed me softly.

I smiled as I pulled away from him, "You can talk to me, you know? I'm a good listener."

He looked down again.

"I saw the coach yell at you before the game, was there a reason?"

He looked at me this time, "You saw that, huh?" He sighed and then hit his steering wheel. I was taken back a little.

"He thinks that my social life is going to interfere with my head again. My father isn't thrilled that I picked now to have a girlfriend now either and apparently talked to the coach about it. I love football, don't get me wrong, but I need something else in my life too," He said turning towards me, grabbing my hand in his, "And I finally found it. I have not stopped smiling since I saw you sitting in home room on the first day. I told myself that I was going to make you mine."

I smiled at him, "I feel the same way, I have never felt this way about a guy. In my old school, I went on one double date and never saw the guy again. There was no spark, nothing clicked. But, the minute you talked to me, I knew you were worth getting to know better."

He leaned over again and kissed me. This time it was deep right away, his tongue quickly found mine as he moaned softly. I responded as I put my hand on his chest, moving up to feel his neck and moving my fingers through his hair. His hand found my thigh I could feel the heat through my jeans. He moved his hand up my back to the back of my neck, reaching into my hair and pulling my clip out to release it. As it fell over my shoulders, he deepened the kiss more. This time I heard my moan escape my lips, never breaking the kiss, his fingers moved through my hair. I started to feel things that I never experienced before. I was so warm, my body felt like a million degrees. His hand moved again to my waist as I felt his fingers reach under my jersey until I felt them on my bare skin. I quickly broke the kiss.

I couldn't breathe, I couldn't speak.

"I'm sorry, I'm so sorry, I lost it again," He said moving back to his seat.

"Don't be sorry, I just know how you are feeling right now, I don't want you to regret anything in the morning."

He smiled at me, "You really do get me already, Emily"

"I really like you, Eric. I don't want to mess this up. But, if you need to focus on football, I'm not going anywhere and I can try to stay out of the way until the season is over."

"No, that's not going to happen. I have never felt like this before and I'm not going to ruin this."

I smiled at him, "Well, you know how I feel, so the ball is in your court."

He leaned back over and kissed me again, "Come on, let's get you home."

We pulled into my driveway, I saw the living room light still on and I knew my mom was waiting up for me.

"So, I have a question for you," I asked him

"Yes."

"Sam was telling me about Homecoming, I know we just started dating so I wasn't sure if you wanted to go with me. I'm assuming you are forced to go because of the football team but I was just curious…" My thoughts trailed off as he grabbed my hand.

"Have I not asked you yet, Emily?"

"Ask me what," I said as I looked into his eyes.

"Emily Stone, would you do me the honor of being my date for Homecoming?"

I smiled at him, "Yes."

He grinned as he leaned over again, kissing me again, a little harder this time. His hand found its way into my hair again as we started to lose control. That deep moan came from my throat again. He responded with his own moan. I broke away just enough, "You are going to kill me."

He laughed softly before putting his lips back on mine. He moved down to kiss my neck softly, the sensation shot right through my body, I whispered softly, "Oh my God." I could feel him smiling against my neck, as his lips moved up to my ear.

"Your skin is so smooth and you taste so good," He said, as I couldn't respond. His lips moved back to mine as I felt his hand reach behind me and move over my ass.

I moaned again, slowly breaking away again, breathing heavily, "I really have to get inside."

"Ok." He said kissing me again softly.

"That isn't helping, Eric."

He smiled as he got out of the car and opened the door for me. He walked me to the door and whispered in my ear, "I will see you in my dreams tonight, Emily." He winked at me as he walked away.

HOMECOMING

The next couple of weeks flew by. I was trying to break up my time by doing my school work, seeing Eric, going to all the games and trying to keep up with my home life that I barely had time to breathe. My mom was having trouble dealing with my father's new baby. He kept calling to share new information with me and I knew my mother could overhear everything. I knew it upset her but I tried my best to keep things light around her. She didn't deserve to be hurt like that.

I even managed to apply to a few colleges. The guidance counselors at school were on my case about not being proactive, so I applied to a few local colleges and even tried my luck with Syracuse.

I also managed to go shopping for Homecoming. Sam, Angie and I went dress shopping after Sam decided to go with Todd. I found a strapless red gown, nothing too fancy and something I thought Eric would like.

Eric. We haven't been able to stay apart from each other. We have been out on several dates; I visit practices, go to the games and enjoy every second I get with him. He had managed to figure out a way to balance football with our relationship so his father hasn't been harassing him too much lately.

I finally met Eric's parents during the week when he invited me to dinner. The entire dinner was very uncomfortable for me. His father kept talking about Eric's future football career. He had a plan for him and nothing was going to stand in his way. I couldn't help but feel guilty that I was monopolizing all his time but Eric kept reassuring me that he had everything under control.

****

I woke up the morning of Homecoming with a smile on my face. It's the first dance that I actually wanted to go to. I jumped out of bed and took my shower, did all the girl stuff and headed back into my bedroom. I looked at the dress hanging in my closet and smiled. He was going to love it.

Sam called about ten times during the course of the day, making sure I was getting ready and wanted to know if I needed help. She was really turning into my best friend.

My mom helped me do my hair, curling it and pulling it back with a fancy clip. I needed to leave some of it down because I knew Eric liked it that way. I slipped on my homecoming dress and called my mom to help me zip up. We both looked in the mirror and smiled.

"You are beautiful, Emily."

"Thanks, Mom. I feel beautiful in this dress."

The dress fell perfectly along my body. The silk red material came down to my knees showing off my legs with the matching high heels.

"Let me get the camera, I know your father would like to see a picture," She tried to smile.

I headed downstairs as I heard Eric pull up the driveway. My heart started to flutter. I wondered if he was really going to like the dress.

My mom looked at me, "Stop shaking, Emily. You are gorgeous." She said as she headed to open the door for Eric.

"Hey Eric, come on in, she's all ready."

"Thanks, Mrs. Stone."

Eric entered the living room and stopped in his tracks, "Just breathtaking."

My mom smiled at him, "Come on kids, stand together, I need pictures."

"Mom, just one."

"Yeah right."

Eric put his arm around me as she took the pictures, he leaned down to whisper in my ear; "You are beautiful."

I blushed softly, "You aren't too bad yourself, Handsome."

We arrived at the high school as he pulled around to the front doors to let me out. He opened the door for me, "I will be right back, Gorgeous," He said as he kissed my cheek and went to park his car.

I headed into the school, hearing the loud music coming from the gym. I saw Sam and Angie inside the gym and they were dancing with the guys. I just smiled at them, glancing over my shoulder for Eric. I waved at Sam and saw Janice starring daggers at me already.

I felt lips on my bare shoulder, as I turned around and saw Eric behind me, "Hey, you ready to have some fun?"

He smiled, "Yep, come on."

We entered the gym hand in hand. His football team quickly gathered around him. I felt his hand slip away from mine as he got mobbed. I looked for Sam and headed over to her. She threw her arms around me and hugged me, "You look fantastic, Emily."

"Thanks, you look great yourself."

"I know, don't I?" She laughed, "I see that you were already left in the wings."

"It's ok, his friends wanted to say hi."

The music changed to a slow song, my friends quickly moved to their dates as the dance floor quickly filled in. I moved until I was on the side of the dance floor. I looked around for Eric but couldn't see him anymore. My eyes adjusted to the dark as I started walking along the bleachers. I finally saw him and stopped in my tracks. He was talking to Janice. She had her hands all over him. I felt the rage build up inside of me, as I saw her look my way. She put her arms around his neck, smiling at me as she continued to talk to him.

I turned quickly and ran out of the gym and entered the cafeteria. I grabbed the closest chair and sat down. I couldn't breathe. I saw Angie and Sam come into the room, "What's wrong?"

I hated feeling like this, it was stupid, "Janice had her hands all over him and it didn't look like he cared, you would think he would have wanted to dance at least the first slow dance with me, right? Why is this bugging me so much?"

"It's bugging you because you really like him. Emily, you know her games. Maybe there is a reason that you don't know about."

"I can't think of anything that would allow her to be all over him like that. I mean, I have barely spoken to him. First, his football friends steal him away then I see that. I think I just want to go home."

"No! You can't," Sam said, "If you are that upset just hang out with us the rest of the night. You look so awesome I bet another guy would dance with you."

I smiled at her, "I don't want to dance with someone else, I want to dance with him."

Angie pouted, "Come on, hang out with Mike and me."

I grabbed her hand and they pulled me back into the gym.

As we entered, I saw Eric talking to his friends again as he managed to get away from Janice. He quickly left them and grabbed my hand from Angie's.

"Where did you go? I wanted to dance with you, Gorgeous," He said looking at me, his smile disappeared, "What's wrong?"

"I saw Janice all over you and don't tell me it was nothing because you didn't stop her."

He didn't say anything at first. He just looked at me, "Emily, please don't get upset. She was just being Janice. You are right though I should have stopped her the minute it happened. I'm sorry."

I just looked at him, getting lost his eyes, "Ok."

He grabbed my hand and walked me over to where my friends were. Sam looked at me and hugged me, whispering in my ear, "You ok?"

I looked at her, "I don't know, maybe."

She pouted, "Come on, this is supposed to be fun."

Angie's date, Mike walked up to me, "Emily, did you want to dance?"

I looked at him and then Eric, well, two could play this game, "Sure."

He reached for my hand and pulled me onto the dance floor, "Angie thought this would put Eric in his place," He laughed.

I smiled at him, "Thanks, it's exactly what he needs."

"I don't know what he problem is, you look beautiful tonight, I wouldn't have left your side at any point."

"Thanks Mike. I appreciate that."

We swayed to the music and every time I moved around I was able to see Eric glaring at Mike. Good, let him be jealous, "Mike, I know this is a lot to ask, but I was wondering if you would mind helping me out a little bit before the song ends."

He smirked at me, "Sure, what's up?"

"I was wondering if you could move your hands a little further down my waist and maybe your head a little more nuzzled into my neck."

He smiled at me, "Oh sure, I will get my ass kicked but if it will make you feel better."

"I promise that he won't touch you."

Mike smirked at me as I felt his hands move lower as he came into my ear and whispered, "How's this?"

My eyes moved across the room and saw Eric jump off the bleachers and move towards the dance floor.

"Perfect."

I felt Mike stop moving, knowing that Eric was right behind me, I pulled slowly away from Mike and turned towards Eric, "Yes?" I asked.

"Can I finish this dance?"

"Sure. Thanks Emily, talk to you later," He said winking at me as he left.

Eric's hands moved around my waist and he pulled me closer to his body, "That won't happen again, I promise. I'm sorry."

I smiled at him, "Well, at least you know how it feels now, right?"

"I thought I was going to lose my mind when I saw his hands move down your dress."

I smirked at him, "Well, I wanted to teach you a lesson. I don't care that you want to be with your friends. I understand there is more to you than just our relationship," I said moving my hands up around his neck and my fingertips moved into his hair, "But, I also don't want you to forget about me."

"Never, Emily. I promise, I messed up and I apologize for that."

I smiled at him, "Ok, you are forgiven then."

He leaned down and lightly kissed my lips as another slow song started. I looked up into his eyes as the night started to improve. He never let his eyes leave mine. I was trying to absorb this moment, not wanting any distractions, but of course, that wasn't going to happen. Out of the corner of my eye, I saw Janice standing with her friends, watching us dance.

I smirked as I looked back to Eric, "Honey, would you do me a huge favor?"

"Anything."

"I feel like I need to prove a point, feel like copying Mike for me and make this dance a little more intimate?"

His lips turned into a sexy grin as he leaned down to my ear as his lips touched it gently, his hands moving right below my waist line. I moved to crush my body tightly against his, my eyes moved across the room, watching Janice's face change. It looked like she was about to cry and I could only smile.

"Are you satisfied?" He whispered into my ear.

"Not quite yet," As I moved my hands up into his hair, moving my lips to his neck and kissing softly.

"You are evil, you know that? Who are you trying to torture, me or her?"

I smirked as the song ended and we walked off the dance floor.

"You two need to get a room," Sam said laughing at us.

The dance ended a lot better than it started. Eric never left my side again. The principal walked up on stage and started talking about the exciting year of football ahead of them. He talked about the team and of course, talked about Eric.

He was starting to get ready to announce the Homecoming King & Queen when Eric leaned down to me, "I know you are going to hate it if Janice is named Queen. What do you want me to do?"

I looked at him, "Don't worry about it. I think I made a statement earlier during our slow dance," I smiled at him as he leaned over and lightly kissed me.

The envelopes were out and the principal was handed the crown for the King. Everyone already knew it was Eric. How could it not be?

He opened the envelope and read off Eric's name. I smiled and clapped for him as he walked up on stage and put his crown on. The entire football team went crazy, cheering for him. He made a small speech and fed into the crowd frenzy. He was such a natural at it. How did I get so lucky?

The principal was then handed the tiara for the Queen and opened the envelope. I turned to Sam, "God help me if she touches him."

"Emily Stone!"

I just stood there; I didn't have any feeling in my legs. I felt Sam pushing me towards the stage, but I didn't hear anything. I was in total shock. I saw Janice quickly leave the front of the gym and exit. Everyone was clapping and cheering as I moved next to Eric on the stage. He grabbed the tiara and slipped it on top of my head. I just stared at him as he got a huge smile on his face.

"I guess it pays off to date the quarterback."

I didn't say anything, I was still shocked. He led me off the stage and down onto the dance floor, as a slow song started.

"I can't believe it," I muttered out.

"I can. Who wouldn't vote for you? You are an incredible person, Emily."

I smiled at him, looking around the room as everyone was watching us dance. I could see Sam and Angie clapping and cheering for me. For the first time, I felt like part of the school and accepted for just being me. This night definitely ended up being the perfect night.

He left me standing outside of the high school with Sam as the guys went to get the cars.

"Congratulations again, you deserve it. I'm so happy for you."

I hugged her again, "Hey, I'm giving you some credit in this, you stood by my side since day one and helped me through everything, so I will share the tiara with you."

She laughed, "Ok!"

I smiled at her as Eric pulled up. He got out of the car and walked over to me, "Ready to go?"

"Yep, I will talk to you tomorrow, Sam," I said as I hugged her again, "And thank you!"

She smiled at me and disappeared with Todd.

Eric opened the passenger door for me and leaned over, "You are so beautiful right now."

I blushed slightly, "You are just saying that, hoping I kiss you good night when I get home," I said winking at him.

He chuckled, "Are you telling me if that I wanted to kiss right now, you wouldn't let me?" He said as his body moved against mine, slightly pushing me against his car.

I lost my train of thought, "I don't know."

He smirked again, "No," He whispered as he moved his face to mine, he wasn't close enough to kiss me, but close enough to feel his breath on my lips.

I was about to give in, when I heard Janice in the background, "Congrats, Eric Honey. You deserve it."

He didn't even turn to acknowledge her I smiled at him, as he never moved away from me.

She walked by us, whispering to her stupid friends, "The bitch didn't though."

Eric quickly backed away from me and turned to her, "Excuse me, Janice?"

"What? What did I say?" She said looking so shocked.

He walked up to her and just looked at her, "Janice, I have been very patient with you, but as of this moment, if you ever talk to her like that again, or even breathe anywhere near her again, it will be your last, do you understand me?"

She just stood there, I quickly went over to him and grabbed his arm, "Come on, Eric, don't even waste your time on her, she isn't worth it."

He turned to me and nodded, as he went back to holding open the door for me and I slipped inside. He moved around the front of the car, I couldn't hear what he said to her, but her face looked miserable.

He took off towards my house, "Thank you for standing up for me back there."

He moved his hand onto my bare knee, I sighed softly, "You don't deserved to be talked to like that. I messed up earlier this evening," he paused, "I told you that wouldn't happen again."

I smiled at him, who wouldn't love to have their boyfriend stand up for them like that. It made me feel wonderful. Maybe it was a little too much, but I didn't care anymore, he stood up for me.

His fingers traced over my knee lightly, I watched them move in the darkness of the car, his radio was softly playing but I couldn't make out what song was on because I was too distracted.

It was the first time he really touched my bare skin, I thought I was going to burst into flames.

He slowly pulled into my driveway and turned the car off. I looked at the house and all the lights were off.

"She didn't wait up for me tonight," I laughed.

He didn't say anything, "You ok?" I asked him.

"Yeah, that just really pissed me off."

"It's over, ok? I've been called worse," I laughed hoping he would smile for me.

He looked at me but there wasn't smile on his face he didn't say anything to me, just stared into my eyes.

"Eric, say something."

"Sorry, just realizing how lucky I am. You look so amazing tonight and when I heard your name called, I was so happy for you. The look on your face was priceless."

I smiled at him, "Yeah, it was definitely a surreal moment for me."

"So, I was wondering something," He softly said to me, "Umm, I'm not sure how to phrase this."

"You can ask me anything, I'm not going to have secrets from you."

He smiled, as his hand moved back to my knee and brushed his fingertips lightly across my thigh. My heart started to race.

"I know you told me that you didn't have a boyfriend in Houston and I was just wondering how far you have gone before."

I blushed, oh no, anything but this conversation. He smiled at me, moving me closer to him.

"I definitely have kissed a guy," I chuckled.

"Is that it?"

I blushed again and turned away from him.

"How is that even possible? Emily, don't be shy around me, I want to know what you thinking right now."

"Feeling a little embarrassed."

"Don't be, I think this makes you so much sexier, you have no idea."

I just sat there feeling his hand move slightly higher up my thigh. The fire just got worse.

He leaned over and kissed my neck softly, "Baby, I'm never going to rush you, we move at your speed, ok?"

I moaned softly feeling his lips on my skin and his hand moving up and down my thigh, "Um, what about you?"

He pulled back leaving his hand on my leg, "Well, I'm a little more experienced. It's pretty easy when every girl in high school wants to be near you and willing to do whatever you want."

I sighed, I was afraid of that answer, "Have you had sex before?"

He stared at me for a minute but didn't respond right away. He grabbed my hand and said, "Yes."

"With Janice?" I asked, so nervous of the answer.

Again, he didn't respond quickly. He just sat there, "No and Emily," He said moving my face to look into his eyes, "It has never been like this with any of them. They were all one time things, nothing special, nothing lasting."

I smiled at him, which made me feel a little bit better.

He leaned over to me again and kissed me harder this time. My hands went up into his hair as I felt him pull me over to sit on his lap. Never breaking the kiss, I felt the steering wheel behind me. I groaned feeling for the first time what I've read about and dreamt about.

He slowly broke the kiss and looked at me, "Are you ok?"

"Yes," I whispered to him. I felt his hands slide up my legs that were on either side of him and underneath my silk dress.

I blushed again and quickly moved back to my seat, "I'm sorry, I can't."

He looked concerned, "I'm sorry, Emily, I wasn't rushing you, I swear."

"I know, I think I better get inside."

"Ok."

He walked me to the door and kissed me good night.

"It was a wonderful evening, Homecoming Queen. Thank you."

SEASONS CHANGE

Homecoming changed my status level at school. Everyone wanted to hang out with me and I was invited to every party under the sun. None of it interested me. I just wanted to draw, hang out with Sam, Angie and mostly, Eric.

That night after Homecoming opened my eyes that I wasn't ready for anything serious yet. In one moment I panicked and ran away with my tail between my legs. I was lucky though, Eric was sticking by my side.

The weeks flew by, between studying and seeing Eric, my days and nights were full. The weather changed fast, the snow was flying and I realized quickly I didn't like it. We were on Christmas break and I was enjoying the time off. I sat in my room drawing, knowing that I should be filling out more college applications. My mom has been on my case trying to lock down my future. I knew I wanted to go to Syracuse so I could be close to Eric but I didn't know if I could afford that. Apparently my father was planning on paying for my education but with the baby due now, I didn't know if that still applied.

I put my drawing pad on the bed and leaned back against the pillows. I thought about Eric. Our relationship had gotten more serious. We talked all the time about our future, we talked about our families, we discussed our dreams and hopes, but I couldn't get past the physical side. I was so scared after Homecoming that I would feel like an idiot with him.

I noticed that I was nervous whenever he kissed me now, I didn't have a reason to be, I knew he was waiting for me to be ready for everything, he wasn't pressuring me but I felt bad. My insecurities were getting the best of me. Maybe I needed a plan to move to the next step. I just didn't know what I should do. I grabbed my laptop and went searching for ideas. I felt like such a nerd, I knew the basics about everything but I needed some reassurance.

As I surfed the web, looking at articles, looking at clothes. I found a lingerie website and was amazed at what was out there. I giggled at myself trying to picture me wearing stuff like that. I definitely don't think I'm ready for that. I laughed again as I heard my door open, I quickly shut my laptop and looked up.

"Hey Gorgeous, your mom said you were up here, so figured I would surprise you." Eric said walking into my room.

Mom never had a problem with him in my room as long as I left the door open, which made me laugh every time. She had nothing to worry about.

"Hey you, I'm trying to keep warm I figured staying in my bed would help with that."

He laughed, "You will get used to it, you haven't seen the worst of it yet, Babe."

I sighed, "Lucky me."

"So, what are you looking at on your computer?"

I blushed quickly, trying to grab my laptop before he could but he was too fast, he grabbed it as he sat next to me on my bed, opening it up.

I wanted to hide underneath my bed and never come out as the website popped up and displayed the sexiest lingerie that I ever seen.

"Wow, Em, anything you want to discuss with me?"

"No, please no."

He laughed and scrolled through the pictures, "Well, if I get a say, I like the black one, but you look hot in red also, but I will leave the choice to you."

"Please God, stop, I'm so embarrassed right now."

"Why, this is hot!"

I threw a pillow over my face and wanted to die.

"Ok, I closed it, it's all over," Eric said moving the pillow off my face, "I'm sorry, but really, what's this all about?"

"Ever since Homecoming, I feel bad. I always stop us when we start getting serious because I know I have no experience and you do. I don't want to disappoint you."

He moved his hand to my face, "Come on, Emily. Are you serious? We have been over this time and time again, I can wait until you are ready. Believe me, when you are ready, you just have to let me know," He laughed, "Wait, were you doing online research?"

I hid under another pillow. I heard him laughing again, "Emily, if you want to know something just ask me, I can always guide you in the right direction. It's not like I have tons of experience but we can figure it out together."

I blushed again as he moved me so I was laying on his chest, "Though I am mad at you now."

I moved to look at him, "What? Why?"

"Now I'm picturing you in one of those outfits!"

This time I laughed, "Good, serves you right for looking at my computer."

He kissed the top of my head, his arms tensed a little bit around me. I felt like he wanted to say something more to me but he didn't.

****

Christmas morning was here before we knew it. I woke up and celebrated with my mom and grandparents. Wrapping paper was scattered all over the floor as things wound down and the clean up process began.

My father called to wish me a Merry Christmas. Beth was doing well dealing with the pregnancy.

"Dad, I miss the warmth, you should see it up here, snow and cold, that's all there is."

He laughed, "Yeah, I remember a few of my visits up there, just have to get used to it."

"Yeah, I guess so. Thanks for the gifts I can't wait to use the art supplies."

"You are welcome. How is the college hunting going? Your mom says you still haven't decided, what's wrong?"

"Nothing, I'm waiting for a reply from Syracuse, but I don't think I can get in. My test scores were kind of low and the tuition is high."

"Emily, don't worry about the money, we will handle it. Why Syracuse though?"

"Well, I guess I have to tell you now, don't be mad. But, I have a boyfriend now, Dad."

"A boyfriend? Emily, you are too young," He said yelling in the phone.

"Dad, I'm eighteen. Stop it. Mom loves him, he's a wonderful guy. He's the quarterback of the football team and has a full scholarship to Syracuse, so I was hoping to go to the same school."

"I still don't approve, I will have to talk to your mother about this. Please just be safe."

"Oh my God, Dad! Please don't start that."

"I'm serious, Emily, I don't want to be a grandfather yet!"

"Jesus Dad, you are about to be a sixty year old father, what's the difference?!" I yelled in the phone, I didn't mean to lose my temper but he was really upsetting me. My mom ran into the kitchen and grabbed the phone from me.

Listening to my parents have a screaming match wasn't a first in my life but it's been awhile. Thinking back to the loud arguments back in Houston, that's when the tears started, great way to spend Christmas morning. I knew that my Grandparents were listening in the other room as my mom slammed the phone down.

"Mom, you ok?" I said I moved to the kitchen table and sat down, hearing the loud noise from the television as my grandparents watched some Christmas special.

"Yeah, he is still as stubborn as he always was. He is threatening to bring you back to Texas if I don't keep my eyes on you. You are a growing woman, Emily, I understand that. I know you and Eric are getting serious, things happen, just promise me before you do anything big, you talk to me."

"Mom, stop it, you know me, I'm the responsible one, so don't worry about me. Dad is being a total jerk. He's on edge and taking it out on us."

"I know. He just brings out the worse in me, I will be ok."

"Sure you will, Mom. You are a very strong person."

She smiled at me, "You think so?"

"Of course, who do you think I'm modeling my life after, huh?"

She looked sad, tears formed in her eyes.

"Mom, what's wrong? That's a good thing!" I said putting my arms around her waist.

"I know, Emily. That means a lot to me."

I smiled at her and kissed her cheek, "Merry Christmas, Mom."

"Merry Christmas, Emily."

Christmas day flew by, dinner with the family, enjoying all my new winter clothes and laughing at the fact that my mom bought me ice skates. It was a broken ankle waiting to happen.

It was around seven at night when the door bell rang. I knew who it was before I got up. Eric was supposed to stop by after all his family stuff was done. I got off the couch and ran to the side door, opening it up and seeing him look so handsome with snow in his hair and a breathtaking smile on his face.

I let him in just enough so he could knock his boots off and I could put my arms around his neck, "Merry Christmas, Eric."

"Merry Christmas, Gorgeous," He said as he lowered his lips to mine.

I heard the clearing of my mom's throat behind us and smiled underneath his kiss. I let go and turned around to face her.

She was smiling at me, "I will let it go because it's Christmas."

"Merry Christmas, Mrs. Stone."

"Same to you, Eric, come inside and I will grab some hot chocolate for you two."

"Thanks, Mom."

Eric and I moved into the living room and sat on the floor by the tree. I reached underneath and grabbed his present.

"I hope you like it I wasn't sure what to get you."

He smiled as he ripped open the paper and opened his gift, "This is awesome." He said as he held up a brand new football jersey of his favorite player, "You are the best girlfriend ever."

I laughed as I heard my mom laugh from the kitchen. She walked into the room and placed the mugs on the coffee table for us. She sat down and watched Eric hand me a small box, wrapped in a pretty red bow.

I took the bow off and opened up the box, inside was a gold necklace with two charms on it. One being a heart and other one a football, I was so taken back, it was beautiful.

"Thank you, Eric." I said wrapping my arms around his neck, "It's beautiful."

I took it out of the box and showed my mom, "Nice job, Eric," She said.

I turned back to Eric after she left, "You want to put it on me?"

He smiled as he opened the clasp and I lifted my hair up. His arms came around me as I felt the necklace take its place around my neck. I felt his lips touch the back of my neck as he turned me back around to see the necklace.

"It looks wonderful on you," He said, "Merry Christmas."

I smiled at him, looking into his eyes, "There is something else I want to share with you."

"What's that?" He said moving so that he sat behind me with his arms wrapped around me.

I grabbed his hands with mine and played with his fingers, "I know it's only been a few months since we started dating but it's been a best time of my life so far. I didn't know what to expect when I moved here, but I quickly found out that it was the best decision I could have made."

"I couldn't agree more," He whispered into my ear, kissing it softly. I loved feeling his embrace around me. I felt so safe in his arms.

I smiled as I turned slightly, so I could see part of his face behind me, his head moved so his eyes could see mine, "I love you, Eric Mason."

I sat patiently as I waited to see panic in his eyes or run screaming from my house, but in my surprise, he opened his lips and whispered, "I love you too, Emily Stone. I have loved you since the moment I saw you in home room, I just didn't know it yet."

I moved my lips to his softly, feeling myself get lost quickly. He parted his lips as our tongues danced with each other. My body turned again so my fingers could run up into his hair. I heard him sigh as he pulled away, "Baby, your mom's in the next room."

"Oh right, sorry," I laughed. I moved back against his chest and smiled.

DECISIONS

The winter months flew by quickly. I wasn't sad about that fact. I was so happy that spring was in full motion and summer was right ahead of us and I was looking forward to graduation. My parents were upset with me because I couldn't decide on a college, I was accepted everywhere so far but my letter from Syracuse hadn't arrived yet and that was the one I was waiting for.

My relationship with Eric was definitely stronger now. We saw each other every night; did our homework together then watched some TV until my mom kicked him out. Our physical relationship improved slightly. I started to move past my fears as we explored our bodies together. He was always a gentleman and stopped when I decided I couldn't go any further.

My father and I had started talking to each other again. His attitude started to get better after he spoke with Eric a few times on the phone, I felt mortified every time he requested to speak with him.

Beth had the baby and I think that helped my Dad to chill out a little. He emailed me pictures of the little bundle of joy. She was definitely adorable, I already felt like a big sister.

As I walked to art class, I knew that Eric would be waiting for me. I smiled as I entered the room and took the seat next to him, "Hey Gorgeous."

"Hey," I said grabbing my pad.

"What's wrong?"

"I still haven't seen anything from Syracuse and I need to make my decision."

He pouted slightly, "Whatever happens we will work it out, ok?"

"Yeah, you say that now, but a few months at your new school, all those girls around you, the new guy on the football team, you will start having new friends," I said not looking at him.

I heard him sigh as class started, "We will talk about this later." I felt his hand run up my leg. I knew he was telling me that everything was going to be ok, but I wasn't sure it would be.

****

I headed back to my locker after class and Sam was waiting for me, "Hey you. Let's have a girls night on Friday, is that ok?"

"Yes. I think that's exactly I what I need."

She smiled, "Good!"

Eric came up behind me and put his arms around me, "Hey Sam, what's going on?"

"Nothing much, I'm stealing your girlfriend on Friday night, sorry to tell you."

"Oh really, why is that?"

"Girls night, no boys allowed," She laughed at him.

I turned to look at him, "You cool with that?"

"Yeah, but we still need to talk, Emily. You aren't going to avoid the conversation."

"I know, we will. I think Sam is going to give me a ride home tonight, too, so you don't have to worry about me."

Eric looked at me with worry on his face, it was the first time since we started dating that he wasn't going to take me home after school.

"Oh, ok, no problem," He kissed my cheek and left to go see his friends.

Sam looked at me, "Ok, what was that about, what is going on with you two?"

"It's nothing, we will talk tomorrow night, come on take me home."

I sat in my room that night just staring at the envelope that I had in my hand. It was addressed from Syracuse University. It was too small to be an acceptance package and I knew that. That's why I couldn't open it. I knew that my life was about to change and I didn't think I could handle it.

I heard a little tap on my door, "Come in."

My mom slipped in the room and sat next to me on the bed, "What's wrong?"

I moved to face her, "I know I didn't get in."

"I'm sorry, Emily. You have been accepted at some other great schools though."

"I know, but they won't have him."

She sighed softly, "I know it hurts, first loves are always painful, but you will see him on holidays and vacations. College is a time to grow into an adult, have fun and learn how life works."

"I know all that, but I have just fallen for him and I thought for sure I had a chance to continue the relationship but now, I know I can't."

"He doesn't want to continue it, honey?"

"No, he does. It's me who knows better. He's going to start his football career, all new friends and all new girls," I sighed.

She chuckled, "Do you trust him?"

"Of course I do."

"Then maybe you should talk to him about this. Just tell him how you feel about it."

"I will."

"Good, because he's downstairs, he looks very worried about you."

I looked at her, "Really?"

"Yeah, do you want me to send him up?"

"Yes. Thanks Mom."

She kissed my cheek and left the room, moments later Eric walked into the room.

"Hey you," He said walking over to the bed and sitting next to me.

"Hey, I'm sorry about earlier, I've just had a lot of my mind today."

"It's ok we have all had bad days. I understand," He said, "What's that?"

I handed him the Syracuse letter, "You can open it I can't face rejection."

He smirked as he opened the letter and read it silently, "Sorry, Baby."

I felt the tears in my eyes. I was expecting it but hearing it was different.

"It's ok I told you I wouldn't get in. Now, I just have to face my worst fears."

He sighed, "We are not breaking up, Emily. Get over it."

"How can you say that? You are going to be three hours away from me, whole new world and all new people, I can't keep you from that."

He brushed his fingers across my cheekbone, as I moved into it.

"Emily, I know it's all going to be new experiences. Whatever college you pick, you will be going through the same things, so why would it make a difference?"

"Because it's you, you are a lot more interesting than I am, don't you understand that? Every girl in the world wants you."

He didn't say anything, we have had this talk before and I don't think he wanted to head down that road again. He moved his fingers up into my hair and pressed his lips hard against mine. He parted them immediately, moaning into my mouth as he pushed me down on my bed, I never felt him this passionate before, his hands slid down my neck, over my arms and rested on my waist. He never let his lips leave mine. I responded with the same passion, my hands moved over his back and moved underneath his shirt. His body melted against mine perfectly, I wound my legs around his waist. Finally he pulled away just enough to let me breathe again.

"I wonder if you will ever understand how much you mean to me and how much I want to be with you."

I looked up into his eyes as my hand moved along his back, feeling his muscles. I loved him so much and I didn't want to lose him.

"Tell me what you are thinking, Emily."

I didn't say anything, I just responded with another passionate kiss. My hand moved down to his waistline and into the top of his jeans. He moaned deeply into my mouth as my leg moved tighter around his waist.

He whispered, "You have got to stop that, your mother is downstairs, Emily."

"I'm tired of stopping."

He didn't wait to respond to that as he kissed me again, his hands moved underneath my shirt and his fingers moved across my hot skin.

He quickly realized what was happening and stopped again, "No, we can't, not here, not now, are you crazy?"

I looked at him, "I'm ready, Eric."

He looked at me, moving his hand off my skin, "No, you're not. You are afraid of losing me and trying to give me what I want so badly."

"Baby, please."

He smirked, "No," As he moved off my body and bed. He walked over to my desk and leaned against it, "You have no idea how bad I want you. It is taking every ounce of strength that I have to not continue this moment, Emily." His breathing was deep and his eyes were extremely dark.

I stared at him with my puppy dog eyes, knowing it would drive him crazy, "Prom then? It's a week away. I will tell my mom I'm staying at Sam's house and we stay at the hotel where the prom is."

He stared at me, "You are just evil. Let me think about it, ok?"

I nodded.

"I better take off, should I pick you up in the morning?"

I got off my bed and found my way into his arms, resting my head against his chest, "Yes please."

"Ok, see you in the morning," He said pulling my face to his and kissing me lightly, "I love you."

"I love you too."

****

Friday night was so much fun with Sam. I spent the evening at her house as we talked about college and boyfriends. We also made plans to go shopping the next day for our prom dresses.

"So, I have a question for you," I said moving to sit on her window seat looking outside enjoying that everything was green again, "Have you had sex yet?"

Sam smiled at me, "Yeah, last year. Todd and I did it after our junior prom."

She was so casual about it, I moved my arms around my knees and put on my head on top of them, "I haven't."

"So? Is Eric pressuring you?"

"No, nothing like that, half the time I'm too nervous to do anything about it. He's been very patient about it."

"Well, that's good. It's no big deal, it was over in like ten minutes and I haven't done it since."

I chuckled, "Ten minutes, huh?"

She laughed, "Yeah, I figure maybe the next time it will be with someone I love or at least lust after a little bit. I think we were both more curious than anything."

"Well, I asked Eric if it could happen after prom next Saturday."

Sam stopped painting her nails and looked at me, "What?"

"You heard me, so I need your help I'm going to sleep over after the prom, ok? I need an alibi."

Sam nodded, "That's fine, but are you sure?"

"Yes, I need to do it before he leaves for college, maybe it will remind him what he has here."

"Emily, that's not a good enough reason. It should be something that just happens. He loves you I see it all over his face you don't need to worry about him."

I just kept looking out her window, I knew she was right but I felt like this was something I had to do. I watched some little kids run down the street as their parents tried to keep up with them. I laughed as the little girl stopped and hugged her father, wondering if that was a future possibility for us. I felt Sam join me on the window seat and put her arms around me, "Stop worrying so much. Come on let's get out of here. We will hit the dress store now before it closes at nine."

I smiled and grabbed my sweater as we headed shopping.

We arrived at the dress shop around eight thirty, the lady looked annoyed that we showed up so late. We convinced her that we were just looking and wouldn't make a mess.

"I want red, Sam." I said as I looked through the racks, "It's his favorite color on me."

"Ok, hang on I'm sure we can find something here."

I dug through the racks and hangers and didn't see anything I liked. I knew I was making this more than it had to be, but if prom night was going to be the night, I needed to look sexy and beautiful.

"Wait, I got it!" She called out and ran over to me with a beautiful red gown. It was strapless, down to the floor, tight fitting and satin. There was small waistline of gems. It was elegant, beautiful and sexy.

"I have to try this on, do you think she will be mad?"

"Not if she wants the sale, come on."

We quickly went into the dressing room and removed my clothes as we slid the dress up and put it into place, it both made us gasp. It was beautiful. I was beautiful.

"Please tell you that you have money, because you need to buy this right now!"

"Yeah, I should be ok," As I looked at the price tag, "He won't be able to resist me now."

"Emily, stop it. You are turning into a horn dog!"

I laughed at her as we started to take the dress off. We went back into the store and I told the lady that she had her final sale of the day. As we headed back to Sam's house, we passed the local hang out and I saw Eric's car.

"You want to stop?" She asked.

"Yes please," I smiled at her as she found a space.

We headed inside and it seemed like everyone from our school was here. I looked around and saw a few more friends and waved, Sam pulled me over to Angie and Mike.

"Hey guys, how's the girls' night coming along?" Angie asked holding onto Mike's hand. They have been dating for a few months now and seem really happy.

"It's great, I found my prom dress!" I said, "It's so awesome."

"That's great, now we just need to find Sam something."

"I will get there, Todd doesn't care what I wear as long as I show a little leg."

I kept scanning the room for Eric, but couldn't find him in the sea of people. Mike looked up at me, "He's in the back with his friends."

I smiled at him, "Thanks, I will be right back."

I moved through the sea of people and headed towards the back of the room, I saw him seating between Chris and Rob and then I saw Janice also at the table. We managed to get through the school year without any more incidents. I honestly don't think I ever spoke another word to her, but seeing her near him still made me feel uneasy.

I walked over to the table, "Hey you."

"Emily! Hey, hang on, let me come over there," He said as he tried to move around another friend at the table, making his friends move from their seats, he finally got to me as I held my arms out for him.

He wrapped his arms around me and kissed me softly, "What are you doing here?"

"Sam and I just bought my prom dress and I saw your car here so I figured I would say hi."

"I'm so happy that you did and congrats on the dress. I can't wait to see it. Is it my favorite color?"

I smirked, "I'm not telling. It's a surprise."

He smiled, "Ok, I can live with that."

"Did you want to go outside and chat for a little bit?"

"Absolutely, come on," He said as he grabbed my hand and started walking through the restaurant with me. He passed Sam and thanked her for bringing me there. She laughed and asked that he wouldn't keep me all night.

When we got outside, we sat on the bench outside of the restaurant.

"Have you thought about my request?" I asked him not knowing what his response would be.

"Yes, a lot."

"And?"

"I need to know more information from you first."

"Like what, Eric?" I asked him gathering his hand with mine.

"I need to know you want to do this because you love me and not because I'm leaving in August and you think it will save our relationship," He said playing with my fingers.

"I love you so much, Eric. I've actually dreamt about it the past several nights, I know it will be wonderful."

"And are you planning on staying with me through college?" He asked looking into my eyes.

"I can promise you that we will have the best summer we possibly can before you leave."

He watched my face his fingers traced my cheekbone, "Ok, we will spend the night together after prom."

I started to blush, "Ok, now I'm nervous."

He laughed, "I better let you get back to Sam or she's going to be mad at me."

I slid my arms around his neck and kissed him, "One week."

He whispered back, "One week."

A NIGHT TO REMEMBER

It was the night of the senior prom. I was finishing up the last minute touches, waiting for the limo to arrive. The dress fit perfectly, my hair was beautiful and I was just waiting for Eric to arrive.

I had talked to Eric last night before going to bed making sure the plan was still on. He said he had taken care of everything and that I would be protected. I was so excited about the evening but also nervous.

I stared into the mirror and smiled. I felt good. I had on my sexy lacy underwear and did my girl stuff and I was ready.

"Emily, your limo has arrived!" My mom yelled up the stairs. I looked in the mirror one last time before grabbing my purse and heading to the stairs. I heard Eric, Sam, Todd, Angie & Mike in the living room talking with my mom.

I started down the stairs and everyone stopped talking. I reached the bottom without tripping over my own feet. I looked up and saw all eyes on me.

"You look amazing, Emily!" Sam said as she came over and hugged me.

"Thanks, Sam, you are beautiful," I said as my eyes moved to Todd, "Not bad, Todd."

"Thanks," He said all macho.

My eyes moved to Eric's, he was just staring at me. It felt like he was trying to read my mind and me his, "You look great, Eric. I love the tux."

He smiled finally moving his lips, "You are beautiful, even more so than I imagined. The color is beautiful on you."

My mom quickly grabbed the camera and made me move into position so she could take a picture of us. Eric grabbed a box and removed my wrist corsage. It had red roses in it to match my dress and smelled wonderful. He gently placed it over my hand and set it into place.

"Come on Emily, stand with Eric," My mom said starting to snap pictures. She took a lot of pictures and I knew she would start crying as soon as we left, I walked over to her and kissed her cheek as we were leaving, "Don't forget I'm at Sam's tonight."

"Right, have a wonderful time tonight guys and be safe," She said shutting the door behind us.

We arrived at our senior prom in fashion. The limo pulled up at the hotel and Eric helped me out and walked in with me hand and hand. I walked through the lobby and headed into the huge ballroom. My eyes scanned the room seeing the huge chandeliers and tables everywhere. It was beautifully decorated with our school colors.

"It looks awesome, doesn't it?" I asked Eric.

"Doesn't hold a candle to you," He smiled kissing my cheek.

I smiled, "Good answer."

We walked around the room and found a table for us and a few friends. We laughed and talked all through dinner. The music played as pictures were taken and everyone was hugging and laughing. As dinner ended, Eric pulled me onto the dance floor as the first slow song played.

"Are you ready for tonight?" He asked me.

"Yes, I am," I said looking into his eyes, "I know that it will be so special."

He smiled at me, that smile that melted my heart every time, "Well, I have the room, it's all ready. Did you want to go see it?"

I looked at him, "Yes!"

We left the prom and headed towards the elevators. As we got to our floor, he pulled the keycard from his jacket pocket and went inside. It was simple but nice. I dropped my purse on the end table and looked around. Eric was staring at me as I explored the room. I finally moved in front of him and draped my arms around his neck.

"Are you happy right now?" I asked him.

"Yes, as long as you are."

"Of course I am this is what I want."

He smiled at me as he leaned down and kissed my lips. I felt the pressure but it was so gentle. His lips moved with mine as they parted. I moaned into his mouth as I felt his hands move down the back of my dress pushing me into his body. He responded to my moan with one of his own. My hands slid under his jacket, I could feel his muscles through his dress shirt.

He stopped briefly, "Baby, we need to go back downstairs, we can't start this right now and you don't know how badly I want to though."

I smirked as my lips moved to his again, I grabbed his hand from my waist and moved it slowly up my body until I placed it on my chest, I felt his body tighten against mine as he deepened the kiss.

He muttered, "Damn you."

I smirked under the kiss as I finally pulled away, "You ready to go back downstairs?"

"Tease."

"I wanted to give you something to look forward to."

I grabbed his hand and my purse and headed back downstairs to see our friends.

We danced the night away, everyone was having a great time. It was the perfect night. Sam and I excused ourselves as we headed to the ladies room. I could feel Eric's eyes burning a hole into the back of me. I knew I had made the right choice deciding that tonight was the night.

Sam and I walked into the fancy hotel ladies room with the crowds of other classmates. We found some privacy at the end of long mirror.

"Are you ready?" Sam asked.

"Yes, we already checked out the room, it's nice."

Sam smiled, "You nervous?"

"Not as much as I thought I would be."

"You need to call me when you get home tomorrow. I want to know everything."

I laughed, "Really? Everything?"

She laughed at me as we touched up our makeup and turned to leave. I saw Janice on the other side of room, glaring at me. I wasn't going to let her ruin my mood as I walked by her and turned to Sam, "Tonight will be the best night of my life."

We returned to the guys, watching the entire football team try to dance. It had to be one of the funniest things I've ever seen. Sam and I headed back to our table to grab something to drink. I watched as Janice entered the ballroom and walked over to Eric. My eyes never left her as she weaved her way through the dance floor and found him. He stopped dancing and turned towards her. Clearly, they were talking about something.

Sam looked at me, "What is that all about?"

"I have no idea but I don't like it, that's for sure," I said as I continued to watch them. She moved her arms around him and before I knew it she was lip-locked with him. My heart stopped immediately. I started to move when Sam grabbed my arm.

"Don't make a scene he's already pushing her away."

I watched Eric say something to her as she smirked and turned around and walked towards me. Eric met my gaze and started after her. As she approached me as she had the nerve to say something to me, "I just had to remind him what my lips felt like, plus give him a memory of our first time." She left as quickly as she came.

I wasn't breathing, I couldn't think straight. Sam pulled out my chair and sat me down. Eric ran over to me and sat in his chair, "Emily, what did she say to you?"

I didn't speak to him I couldn't find the words that I was looking for. He lied to me. He's been lying to me since we started dating. He had slept with Janice. Janice!

"Emily, please talk to me," He begged me.

"You tell me, what do you think she said?"

He looked into my eyes, the tears were starting and he knew.

I whispered to him, "Why did you lie to me?"

"You are so innocent, I was falling in love with you, I wanted you to be comfortable with me and I knew how you felt about her,"

"You lied to me, Eric."

"I know, I'm so sorry," He reached for my hand and I moved it away quickly, "Please don't be like this. We have such a great evening planned and this time I'm in love, it's going to mean so much more to me."

"You mean we *had* a great evening planned, I never want to see you again, Eric, its over."

"No Emily, I'm not letting you leave me like this, please."

Just as I was about to leave the ballroom, the principal headed to the stage to announce Prom King and Queen. My eyes quickly found Eric's and I couldn't stop crying. Sam grabbed my arm and pulled me off to the side.

"Emily, you know that you and Eric are going to win, right? What are you going to do?"

I didn't have an answer for her, I couldn't stop crying. I was barely paying attention as the principal read through his speech. I heard the class erupt in cheers as they called Eric up on stage to receive his crown. My heart sunk into my chest as I looked at Sam, "I don't know what to do."

Sam hugged me, "Just go up there, get your tiara and do your dance. We will leave as soon as it's over. I promise, Emily." I nodded as we made our way closer to the stage.

I looked up at Eric, who was staring at me. I could tell he wanted to talk to me and I could see the hurt on his face. I saw the principal open the envelope and call my name. I just stood there, feeling Sam's arm go around my waist and give me a push.

I slowly walked up the stairs and moved next to Eric as he put the tiara on my head, never breaking eye contact with me. He grabbed my hand as we moved to the dance floor, his arms wrapped tight around me. My body wasn't responded, I didn't want to be here, all these eyes on me, not realizing how badly I wanted to run away and hide from the world.

"Emily, please listen to me. I don't want to lose you. Please listen to me." Eric begged as he tried to make me dance.

My legs weren't moving and I could feel everyone staring at me, "I can't do this. I can't be here. Sorry." I said as I ran out the door and directly outside. The air had cooled down and I tried to calm down but the tears wouldn't stop. I felt like my world had come crashing down.

GRADUATION

The week after prom was the hardest, avoiding Eric at school was next to impossible. We were the talk of the school and everywhere I went, I felt people staring at me. He was everywhere and every time I saw him, he wanted to talk to me, beg me to come back to him. I always managed to work my way out of the conversation and go the other direction.

Graduation was only a few days away. Finals were nearing an end and summer was here. I had picked my college and decided to go to the University of Buffalo. My mom was having a hard time lately since my dad was in town and I knew she loved having me around so I figured I would be close by in case she needed me. I managed to get into the dorms at the last minute and requested Sam as my roommate. We were both excited that we would be living together.

When I got home, my mom was making dinner already as she gave me a quick hug and asked how my finals went.

"Good, I'm officially done with high school, just need to get that diploma," I said smiling at her.

"Great! Have you talked to Eric yet?"

"Mom, we have been over this, it's over between us."

She didn't mention it again, she knew it upset me. She was there when I cried myself to sleep every night. She just hoped that I would listen to him and give him another chance. But, she didn't know the real story; she didn't know how much he broke my heart by lying to me.

I snapped out of it when I heard the doorbell, "You expecting Dad tonight?"

"I hope not, I'm in no mood for him or that bimbo."

I laughed at her as I went to the door and opened it.

Eric.

"What do you want? It's not a good time."

"Please, give me five minutes," He said, "Please."

I walked out the door and shut it behind me, I had a feeling that I didn't need my mother to hear this conversation.

"Five minutes."

"I just wanted to say that I was sorry again," He said walking into my garage after me.

"I've heard this before, don't you have anything new to say."

He stared at me, "You know this is a place that I hold dear to my heart, this was the place that I realized that you were mine after you kissed me that way."

I blushed lightly thinking back to the beginning of the school year on that wonderful Sunday morning.

"If I only knew what you were, you wouldn't have gotten so lucky."

He sighed, "Please Emily. I know I was wrong. There were so many times when we were talking about it that I wanted to tell you the truth but could never think of the right words."

"It's easy, hey Emily, I slept with Janice, you know, that girl that you hate so much."

He grabbed my hand tightly, "I regret not telling you, Emily, I swear, I feel so horrible that I ruined our prom night, I have to live with that, but I don't want to live knowing that you hate me."

"I don't hate you, I just can't be with you, Eric," I said as I started to walk away, he grabbed me and pulled me into his arms, his lips were quickly pressed against mine. It was passionate as I responded, tasting him again. I sighed as I realized how much I missed kissing him. Finally, I snapped back to reality.

"No, no, you can't make it all go away by kissing me, Eric," I said wiping my lips, "I hope you have a wonderful college experience, I don't wish you any ill will, please realize it's over."

I left him standing in the garage as I turned away from him.

****

Graduation morning arrived. I was so excited, I was done with high school and I just needed that piece of paper. My father and Beth were going to meet us at school, which made my mom happy.

I put on the red summer dress that I bought last night and finished my hair, smoothed out the dress and grabbed my heels.

I heard my mom enter the room behind me, "Red, huh? You aren't trying to be mean, are you?"

"No Mom, I just like this color on me. I could care less if he looks my way today."

"Emily, I just wish you would tell me what he did, maybe I can help. It's your graduation day, I just want you to be happy and enjoy it."

"Mom, I'm thrilled. I'm in a great place, look how amazing I look," I laughed as I kissed her cheek, "Come on let's head over to school." I grabbed my gown and cap and headed downstairs.

We got to school and found my Dad, "Hey guys," I said as I grabbed my little baby sister, "I'm so happy that you can see me graduate, even though you have no idea what's going on."

Everyone laughed as I put her back into her stroller. My dad hugged me and smiled, "I'm so proud of you today, Emily."

"Thanks Dad. It feels good that I'm moving into another chapter of my life now."

He smiled, "Your mom told me about you and Eric. I'm sorry that it didn't work out. She said that you took it very hard."

"Yeah, it was rough, but I'm fine now," I smiled as I saw Eric's parents enter the gym. He must be close behind.

"Ok, I should go get ready and find my friends. I will see everyone after I have the diploma."

Everyone hugged me even Beth. I kissed my little sister good bye and headed out the gym doors and into the cafeteria where everyone was getting ready. I found Sam and Angie laughing at our lunch table as I headed over to talk to them. They jumped up and hugged me.

"We're done, Em! I'm so happy that high school is over!"

I laughed as I helped Angie get her cap on, "I know the feeling," I said as I looked around the room, my eyes caught his eyes. He was staring at me.

Sam came over and grabbed my cap, "He's been looking at you the entire time, Emily. You wore that color on purpose, you are cruel and heartless."

I laughed leaving his gaze, "I did not, I just love this dress." She laughed as she helped me put the cap on and I zipped up my gown, "I need some water, be right back."

I walked over to the table that had bottles of water on it and grabbed one as I turned around, I ran right into him. Memories of the first day of school came flooding back to me.

"Congratulations, Eric."

"Same to you, Emily, you look amazing today."

"Thank you. Well, have fun at Syracuse, see you around," I said as I started to leave. I felt his hand grab my arm. I looked back at him.

"I'll ask one more time, Emily, please forgive me and come back to me. I can't stop thinking about you; I'm still in love with you."

I just looked at him I didn't know what to say anymore. "You already know my answer to that, Eric."

"I will win you back, Emily. I promise you that, you are my life. We are all entitled to a few mistakes. I made mine and I promise I will never make another one again."

I looked at him as he grabbed my hand, "Eric, go get dressed, your parents are waiting to see you graduate."

"Emily, tell me you don't love me anymore and I will never say another word to you."

I looked away from him and saw Sam and Angie watching us, "Eric, I will love you until the day I die. You will always be my first love."

He smiled at me as he pulled me back to him, "Then come back to me, Emily, I can be your first and last love."

"I can't, I'm sorry, you broke my heart and it's still not mended," I said as I walked away from him.

During the ceremony, I kept looking over at him and wanted to cry. This year started out so scary, leaving my home in Texas, moving to a new city and starting over. I was so lucky to find Sam and Angie on my first day, they really have become close friends of mine and I hope we always have that connection. I sat and watched my classmates move across the stage as they grabbed their diplomas and seeing them so happy to start the next chapter in their lives was exciting to see.

As they got to Eric, I watched him smile and wave at his family. He quickly found my eyes and winked at me which made me smile back at him. I was proud of him. He's starting his football career and his new life. He was destined to make it big, part of me was sad that I wouldn't be experiencing it with him. I snapped out of my trance as I heard my name being called out; I got up and walked the stage getting my diploma. I heard my family and friends cheering as I finished my high school career.

After graduation, I found Sam and Angie and gave them quick hugs. Promising Angie that we wouldn't lose touch as she headed off to NYU and making her promise that I get to be a bridesmaid when Mike pops the question. She laughed as I turned to find my family. I almost ran right into him as my hands came up and fell against his chest.

"Sorry Eric, I didn't see you there."

He smiled, "It's ok, congrats on your diploma."

I smiled at him, looking into his eyes, "You too, well I should go find my family, good luck again at Syracuse, I know I will be hearing about you in the future." I said as I walked away from him for the last time that summer.

COLLEGE

Sam and I spent every day together buying things for our dorm room. We were so excited to be starting college. We went to the campus a few times and walked around trying to figure out where things were. It was a beautiful sunny day in Buffalo when we got our room assignment and decided to walk campus to find the building.

"This is going to be so exciting, new life, new classes, new experience and new boys!" Sam laughed, "College boys!"

I laughed, "I'm not sure if I'm ready for that, but I'm still excited."

She looked at me as we kept looking for the building, "Have you seen him at all this summer?"

"No, my mom said he has already left for Syracuse, the football program has already started."

"Are you sorry that you didn't make up with him before he left?"

"No, he broke my heart, I don't know if I will ever get over that."

She nodded, "Ok, back to happier things. Let's try to find this building."

We kept walking, finally finding our dorm building. The doors were locked but at least we were able to figure out where stuff was from there.

"This is going to be the best year," Sam said. She had the biggest smile on his face when she turned and saw two guys staring at us.

"Sam, come on, we haven't even started here yet and you are already picking up guys, give me a break."

She laughed, "College men, Emily, College men!"

She started walking over to them with me close behind, I whispered, "You are out of control."

"Hi," She said, "Do you guys go here?"

"Yeah we are juniors, you?"

"Just little freshman, trying to figure out where everything is," She flirted like a pro.

I laughed out loud and everyone turned to look at me, "Sorry, hi."

The one guy smiled at me, "So, what's your major?"

"Graphic Design, you?"

"Communication; we are actually both on the football team."

My heart sunk into my chest as Sam looked at me. She knew what I was thinking about and who I was thinking about.

"We were about to head down to the field for practice, would you guys like to come down and watch the Bulls at work?" The taller dark haired one asked.

I shook my head quickly, "Sorry, we need to go."

Sam pouted, "Sorry guys, maybe next time."

I quickly turned and started to walk away.

****

It was already mid October, classes were in full swing, adjusting to dorm life finally sunk in and Sam had a different guy every week. I was deep into my graphic design classes, staying late after classes, working in the lab trying to learn every thing that I could.

I made it home every weekend to see my mom; she started dating someone which made me feel wonderful. She was finally moving on. We had Sunday dinner every week and Paul was starting to join us.

"Honey, can you help me in the kitchen?" My mom yelled for me.

I left Paul to the football game in the living room and headed to see my mom.

"I'm just about done with sauce," She said handing me the spoon, "Keep stirring. So, what do you think of Paul?"

"He's really nice, Mom. I like him."

She smiled at me, "Good, I'm glad you think that way."

"I can see that look in your eyes, Mom. You are falling for him!"

"Shhhhh, he can't hear that."

I laughed, "Mom, you are so funny, you look like I did when you talked to me about…" My thoughts trailed off, I made myself try to forget him. Whenever he popped into my mind it made me believe that I had to start all over again.

I didn't hear my mom walk over to me but I felt her arms around my shoulders, "Emily, are you sure you want it to be over with Eric?"

I cringed at his name, "Yes, it needs to be. He lied to me."

"I know you didn't want to share the whole story with me, which I understand, but I see it on your face, I see that you still love him, Emily."

"I'm over it, Mom." I said moving back to the sauce and turned off the heat, "Let's have dinner, go get Paul."

She smiled at me as she grabbed the bowl, "Maybe just call him, Emily. His mother left me his phone number, just in case."

I looked at her, "What?"

"You know that we are friends, we talked about how horrible it was that you guys broke up, so we always had hopes that maybe your paths would cross again, so I gave her your number and I'm now giving you his."

"Well, I'm assuming since I haven't heard from him, he has given up on it too."

"You don't know he has your number to begin with and he's probably just as stubborn as you are!" She grabbed the food and left the room.

I got back to the dorm around eight and Sam was curled up on her bed with her English assignment.

"Hey! How was Sunday dinner with the family?"

"It was nice, Mom's boyfriend is really cool. He's good for her."

"That's nice," She smiled.

"What's wrong with you?" I asked her as I took my coat off and changed into my pajamas.

"Nothing, just stressing about a few classes, midterms are around the corner."

"Yeah, I know. But, if you need help studying I will help you."

"Thanks, grab this sheet and ask me the questions."

We studied for the next few hours until she fell asleep. I laughed when she didn't answer the last question as I noticed her passed out on pillow. I grabbed her blanket and covered her up and grabbed my laptop.

I started to think about Eric, wondering if he was dating, how football was going for him, did he ever think about me? My plans didn't work out the way I wanted them to for us. I thought by now we would be trying to manage a long distance relationship and of course, would have already spent the evening together. I started to get angrier, the more I thought about it. I took a deep breath and typed in the Syracuse University website.

I wasn't sure what I was looking for or what I was doing. Maybe I was trying to reach out. I looked over the pictures from the football games; it looked like quite the event. The stands were full of orange sweatshirts and people going crazy for their team. As

I scanned the page, I found him. The picture wasn't great, but he was on the field in his practice jersey. He looked amazing. I clicked on the picture and saved it on my computer. Above the picture was a link for the upcoming games. I hesitated but clicked shortly after. This Saturday night was another game and it was only a three hour drive. I smiled slightly, thinking about seeing him again.

I looked over at Sam sleeping, "Sam, wake up!"

She moved her head towards me, "What? It can't be morning yet."

"No, it's one in the morning."

"Then why are you talking to me?"

"How do you feel about a road trip on Saturday?"

"Road trip? Where are we going?" She asked, wiping her eyes and looking at me.

"Syracuse."

She didn't say anything at first. She stared at me wondering if she was still asleep, "Let's go!"

SYRACUSE

We left around noon, hoping to get there early enough to look around. My mom was thrilled about the road trip. I took his number just in case I got the nerve to call him. I had no idea what I was going to say to him when I saw him. I honestly had no right to even go see him. I was the one who broke it off. I sighed but realized this is what I needed to do. Maybe I could at least leave with my friend again.

We found a parking spot at the stadium and watched in amazement as the crowds were already there celebrating and looking forward to that evenings game.

"Well, Todd gave me Eric's room number if you wanted to take a chance that he is there."

"I don't know, I don't want to bug him, maybe we will just walk around for a bit and see the campus."

"That's fine. Whatever you want, I know you are worried, Em. I see it on your face, but you are taken the first step today to get him back. You look amazing. So, stop worrying!"

I laughed at her, though, I did agree, I looked good. I grabbed my jeans that he loved on me, my cute red t-shirt and even cut my hair.

We started walking around campus amazed by the size of it. There was a different atmosphere here, it was electric. Sam was enjoying herself watching all the Syracuse men, I laughed every time she wanted to stop and stare.

We ended up down at the athlete center. My breathing stopped when I saw a bunch of guys hanging around in football jerseys. I sat at the nearest bench and watched. Sam sat next to me, "I have an idea but are you sure you want see him?"

I thought about the question first, I had decided that I would reach out to him but now I wonder if I made the right choice. I still loved him, I had tried to bury it deep down inside of me and move on but I couldn't. I still believed that somehow we were supposed to be in each other's life. I slowly nodded at Sam.

"OK," She said as she left my side. I watched her approach the football guys, flirting with the best of them. She was amazing. She laughed when she needed too and touched the arms of a few of them. They were putty in her hands. I saw her turn around and head towards the building as she looked back at me and winked.

I didn't know if I should follow her and stay here. She was up to something but I didn't know what it was. I stood up when I saw her come out of the building, my breathing stopped. He was right behind her, she pointed my way and his gaze followed. Our eyes locked as a small smile appeared on his face.

They headed my way, "Emily, look who I found?"

I watched as Eric came in front of me, he put his arms out and I gave him a quick hug.

Sam smiled, "I'm going back to talk to my new friends."

I looked back at Eric, "Hi Stranger."

"Hey, I can't believe you are here."

"Yeah, it was a last minute kind of thing."

"You should have called, I could have gotten you tickets by the field or something," He said sitting down next to me.

"Like I said last minute; I was talking to my mom and she mentioned that maybe it was time that I forgave you and I guess I agreed."

He smiled, "Yeah, I know our mom's have been talking a lot lately. I have a feeling the depression in their children might have something to do with it."

"Have you been depressed, Eric?"

"Since the minute you left me at Senior Prom."

I looked at him again I didn't know how to approach this at all. I was hoping that when I saw him it would all come to me but it wasn't, "Yeah that was the worse night of my life."

"You and me both and that definitely was not my plan for the evening," He laughed.

"So, are you dating here?"

He paused before answering, "I've been on a few dates," He reached over and took my hand, "But, I haven't connected with anyone like I did with you."

I smiled, happy to hear he's being honest with me, "How do you like school?"

"It's great, classes are good. Football is a lot tougher here," He laughed, "I'm still on the practice squad but Coach says that I'm making great progress."

"That's great, Eric. I'm happy for you."

"What about you? Who's the incredibly lucky guy back in Buffalo?" He asked smiling at me.

I laughed, "I'm single, haven't been on a date since Senior Prom."

He stared at me, "Really?"

"Yeah, you broke my heart, Eric."

He sighed, "I will never forgive myself for that, Emily. You shouldn't have found out that way."

I didn't say anything to him I just stared at his face, trying to remember every detail for when I had to leave him later.

"So, you are coming to the game, then?"

"Yeah, we managed to get nosebleed seats," I smiled.

"Are you staying in Syracuse tonight?"

"We wanted to but couldn't find anywhere to stay."

"Yeah, game days are normally intense around here. I don't want you to leave though."

I smiled, "Sorry. We figured we should leave right after the game."

He grabbed her hand again, "Please stay."

"Eric, unless we sleep in our car, we can't."

He looked at me, "Stay in my room."

"Don't you have a roommate?"

"He goes home every weekend," He said as he moved closer to me on the bench, "Please."

"I have Sam with me."

"So, she can sleep in his bed," He said trying to read my face.

I didn't say anything, I wasn't sure if I was ready for this, I just came to talk to him. I quickly scanned the area for Sam. I found her standing by her new friends.

I looked back at Eric, "I will be right back."

I headed over to see Sam, "Hey Emily. I want you to meet Rob and Aaron. They are on the football team too."

"Hey guys, can I steal Sam away just for a second?"

"Are you sure you don't want to stay and chat with us? We offered to take Sam out tonight after the game, we could always bring you along too, Sweetie," The tall one said grabbing my arm.

"I don't think so, but thanks for the offer though," I said as I tried to pull my arm away. His grip wasn't letting me go though.

"Come on, Emily, one drink."

I didn't have time to respond, Eric was by my side, "Let go of her, Aaron."

"Hey Eric, we were just getting to know each other."

"She's mine so if you would kindly remove your fingers from her arm before I will remove them for you."

I smirked at Eric, hearing those words sent shivers through my body. I felt his hand disappear off my skin. Eric put his arm around my shoulders and stared at Aaron.

"Sorry Man, I didn't know."

Eric just nodded at him. I felt the tension in his arm. It felt so good to feel his arm around me again, I found myself leaning towards him.

"Sam, can we chat?" I asked her.

"Sure, come on."

Sam and I headed back to the bench as Eric followed behind us. "What would you think about spending the night here?"

"I would love to but we couldn't find a hotel."

"What if I found us a room?"

"Where?" She asked as I turned around and stared at Eric, "OH!"

"Yeah, his roommate is out of town and we can stay in his room."

Sam leaned over to me, "Are you going to sleep with him!"

"NO! Of course not, just thought it would be fun, I realized that I really miss him."

"I would do anything for you, Emily," She said as she hugged me.

"Thanks Sam, I owe you one," I turned towards Eric and realized he was right behind me.

"Yeah Sam, we owe you one," He said looking into my eyes his arm went back around my shoulder.

We headed back towards the sports arena since Eric needed to meet the team to get ready for the game. We agreed to meet at the front gates after the game so we could head back to his dorm with him.

Eric leaned over and whispered to me as Sam was quickly distracted by more football players, "I can't wait to hold you in my arms all night long."

I smiled at him, "I've dreamt of that so many times."

"Me too, Emily. So, does this mean you want to try our relationship again? No lies, no secrets. Just us."

I looked into his eyes I wanted to believe that so much. I wanted our relationship back. After looking at all the college guys no one even came close to Eric. I missed his touch, I missed his smell and I missed everything about him. Just say yes, Emily. Stop staring at him and say yes.

Eric moved a little closer to me, "Well?"

"Yes," I softly said.

He smiled at me, leaning down kissing my lips. All the emotions came flooding back to me. My hand moved up into his hair as he deepened the kiss. I sensed that he was feeling the same emotions as he held my face against his. I let out a soft moan, as he pulled away and whispered, "God I missed that."

I smiled as I heard Sam behind us, "You guys are making me sick again, get a room!" I heard her giggling.

Eric whispered, "Tonight."

The game was so exciting. Sam and I cheered on Syracuse with the thousands of other screaming fans. The stadium was filled with Orangemen. It was an awesome sight as I watched the field and saw Eric on the sidelines discussing plays with the starting quarterback. He looked like he was enjoying himself. I could tell he was in his element. I stared around the stadium and could understand why this meant so much to him. I sat back down as the other team came onto the field. I just smiled as I enjoyed the night.

"So, what's the plan for tonight, Em?" Sam asked.

"I guess we will grab some dinner and hang out at his room," I said looking at her, "I'm not sure."

"Well, I was thinking about hanging out with Rob, we started to really connect."

"I don't know, Sam. You barely know him I don't want you to going off by yourself."

Sam laughed, "Are you my mom?"

"No, I just love you, I don't know this guy," I said putting my arm around her. She laughed at me again.

As the game ended we headed back to the athletic center and waited for Eric. I watched as all the people poured out of the stadium; I turned to see Rob come from the building first. Sam started to smile. I looked at her and rolled my eyes.

"Hey ladies," He said as he came up to Sam, "What's going on tonight?"

"Nothing much, just waiting for Eric, guess we are hanging out with him tonight," Sam said putting her hand on his arm.

"Well, there is a party at The Hub tonight, if you guys wanted to come. Normally it's a pretty good time after a game," Rob said as Eric came up behind him.

I smiled as he came over by my side and kissed my cheek, "Hey you, congrats on the win."

"Thanks, so what's going on?" He asked.

"Well, Rob invited us to The Hub and I think that Sam wants to go," I winked at her.

Eric laughed, "It's a great party, but I sort of wanted some private time tonight with you."

"Well, why don't I take Sam for a few hours and you and Emily can get reunited," Rob said as he put his arm around Sam.

Eric smiled, "Sounds like a plan to me, we will see you later back at my room."

"Great!" Sam said as she hugged me and ran off with Rob.

"So, should I be worried about your friend, Rob?" I asked.

"Not at all, he's one of the good guys," Eric said wrapping his arm around me and walking back to his dorm room.

Eric and his roommate decorated a little bit, nothing like Sam and I though. The walls had posters of sports and some almost naked woman, I saw Eric blushing a little; "It's my roommates."

I laughed and nodded my head, "Sure it is."

I continued to look at his side of the room, the books were all over his desk and his bed wasn't made. He had football stuff everywhere as I sat on his bed and looked at the small table next to the pillow. I saw a small picture of us from senior prom. The picture was taken before all the chaos broke out. I picked it up and looked at him.

"I told you I wouldn't forget about you when I left for college. You are with me all the time, Emily," He sat next to me on the bed, "That picture reminds me of my horrible mistake, I will live with that forever."

I looked back at the picture, that moment felt like it happened so long ago. I was smiling in the picture, my arms were around his waist, I thought that we were going to share the most imitate moment with each other.

Eric moved his arm around me and pulled me closer to him. I put the picture back on his nightstand and turned to him, "So, do you think about me?"

"Yes, everyday. You are still the love of my life, Emily. That will never change."

"My mom has been trying to get me to call you since our break up. I never told her the real reason behind everything but she wanted me happy again and she knew that meant at least calling you."

"Yeah, my mom was the same way. She gave me your phone number but I couldn't dial. I was so afraid you would just hang up on me or Sam wouldn't let me talk to you."

I laughed, "You are so wrong about that. Sam has been pulling for us since June. She wouldn't stop talking about you. Eric this, Eric that, call Eric."

He smiled at me, "I should have, I'm sorry."

"Don't say you're sorry, I had your phone number too and I didn't pick up the phone either. Instead I drove three hours in hope of getting a glimpse of you," I laughed as I looked into his eyes. They were different, they were darker than normally. He had a look on his face that I hadn't seen before.

He leaned over as his lips pressed against mine. I missed that feeling. Our lips quickly parted as our tongues found each other, my hand slid up into his hair as he pressed his lips tighter to mine. I felt him moving us as he moved to lay on top of me, feeling his body press against mine. It was a different feeling, no one was going to barge in on us and no one was around to interrupt us. We gave into each other.

His hands moved along my body and underneath my t-shirt, I felt his heat of his hands burning against my skin as his fingers moved over my stomach and worked higher up my body. I moaned into his mouth as my hands moved underneath his shirt. I felt him pull away just enough to mutter, "I've missed you so much, Baby."

I couldn't think of any words to say to him, my body responded for me as my lips moved to his neck, tasting him again. He responded with a moan, as his eyes closed and moved his body tighter against mine.

"Are you sure, Emily?" He asked me in between kisses. I don't remember how or when he did it, but I felt my jeans open and my t-shirt was almost off.

I had to answer him but I didn't know how. Of course, the answer was yes. I grabbed his shirt and pulled it over his head, staring at the strongest ab muscles I've ever seen. My fingers traced over all the ridges. My t-shirt followed his onto the floor. He sighed softly as his lips moved to the top of my breasts. I moaned, my head tilting back as his fingers moved down my stomach to my jeans.

"You are so beautiful, Emily," He said pulling my jeans further down my legs until they were gone. I was feeling things that I never felt before. The heat ripped through my body, I never realized it would be this intense.

He grabbed my legs and moved them apart and around his waist as he moved over me. His lips were so passionate against mine. I didn't feel nervous, my body was responding to his every touch.

"Are you sure, Emily?"

"Yes, please, don't stop now."

He smiled as he took precautions to make me safe. The minute it happened, my world exploded. I was experiencing something that I didn't know I could. His body moved with mine and kept saying how much I loved him and he kept saying it back to me. My nails dug into his back as I entered an existence that I never knew was there.

SLEEP OVER

It was around midnight when I finally woke up and felt his arms around me. I was naked by his side and I never felt better than I did right there. It felt so perfect like the stars finally aligned for us.

I turned over so I could face him, his eyes were open and he smiled at me, "Hey Sleepyhead."

I smiled back, "Hey Sexy."

"Sexy, huh?

"Thank you for best night of my life, Eric. I mean that. I think it was suppose to happen like this. It couldn't have felt more right."

He smiled and kissed me lightly, "I couldn't agree more."

I moved closer to him as our bodies paired up again, I kissed his neck as I felt his arms around me tighten, "You make me crazy, Em."

I smiled as I heard a knock on the door, "Oh crap!"

We both jumped out of bed and grabbed for our clothes laughing. It felt like Mom and Dad just got home and we were caught. I watched his body as he threw a pair of sweatpants on. He was gorgeous. I made sure everything was in place as he opened the door. Sam and Rob came walking in. Sam quickly looked at me and laughed, "What's going on, guys?"

We both blushed as Rob spoke up, "I think Eric just got laid!" I turned bright red as I ran out the door and into the bathroom. I wasn't alone for long as Sam came in right after me.

"Emily! You slept with him!"

I nodded as tears filled my eyes.

"What's wrong? I thought you would be happy," She said hugging me.

"I am happy, very happy, but hearing Rob say that made me feel very self aware. Is it that obvious?"

Sam laughed, "Well, let's see, you are glowing, you guys took forever to answer the door and Eric is barely dressed. You put the pieces together."

I laughed this time as I went to the sink and washed my face, "It was amazing, Sam. It was just amazing."

She hugged me again, "I'm so happy that he was your first. It means something now. You guys deserve each other and it's about time you realize that."

I smiled, "It was so intense. Don't get me wrong, painful at first, but he was so patient and it just worked. I want to see him again, is it safe to go back?"

Sam nodded, "Rob is great, I'm sure he feels bad."

"Wait! How did it go?"

Sam smiled, "It was a lot of fun. These people know how to party! Rob is so nice he never left my side all night. I think I met most of the football team. He invited me to come back for the next game and I invited him to Buffalo, he said he may try to come home some time with Eric. He's from New York City though."

I smiled as I listened to her, she sounded different. She's never this bubbly about a guy. Normally, she just did her thing, but this time she is getting to know him. I was impressed.

We opened up the bathroom door and I quickly saw Eric standing against the wall. He managed to find a t-shirt unfortunately.

He moved his arms around my waist, "You ok?"

I nodded, "Yeah, sorry about that, emotions are running high apparently"

He smiled, "I'm sorry about Rob, I made him wait so he could apologize to you."

I laughed, "It's ok, Sam told me that it was pretty obvious."

He blushed this time as he walked me back to his room with Sam following us. Rob was waiting on his roommate's bed for us, "Emily, I'm so sorry. I'm normally not that loud but I guess I'm still all pumped up after the party."

I smiled, "It's ok, really."

Eric wrapped his arms around me as we all started talking. It was after two when Rob finally left. It was so cute watching Sam saying good bye to him. I hoped that Eric and I weren't that annoying when we started our relationship.

Sam curled up on his roommate's bed and was quickly asleep. I moved close to Eric as he pulled the comforter over us. "So, are you happy about tonight?" He whispered in my ear.

I turned to face him, "Yes, if it's possible, I love you even more right now."

"I feel the same way, Em," He said as he moved a piece of hair behind my ear, "I don't want to let you go in the morning."

I pouted, "I don't know if I can leave you now."

He kissed my pout, "You will but only because I'm coming home in a week for fall break."

I smiled at him as my lips touched his. It was innocent at first but quickly changed to passionate. I whispered, "Baby, Sam is right over there."

He smirked at me, "So, how quiet can you be?"

I looked at him through the darken room, "You tell me."

He laughed, "Good point, but I can't help myself I need you again before you leave me."

"Eric, I can't, not with her here. You will just need to wait until you come home."

His hand quietly moved under my shirt, I felt the heat building already, I could already sense when his body was ready. His breathing was heavier as I moved my hand down his abs and into his sweatpants, he moaned in my ear, "Don't tease me, Emily."

I smiled against his neck as I kissed it, "Your breathing is getting deeper, Baby, you ok?" I smirked as I tried to control the situation.

"No, you are driving me crazy, Emily I swear we will be quiet."

For a moment I lost my mind and said ok. The moment was as beautiful as the first one. I tried to control myself because of Sam in the next bed. I heard her snoring, so I knew we were ok.

Our bodies collapsed together as Eric moved from the bed quietly as he went to take care of things. Tomorrow morning was going to be very rough when I had to leave him. My body was still at peace as I slipped Eric's shorts on and grabbed his t-shirt, I had already fallen asleep when he crawled back into bed.

Just as I thought, the next morning was horrible. Sam and I got up, showered and Eric fed us before we had to leave. I couldn't leave his embrace, we leaned against the car as Rob said good bye to Sam. I couldn't control my emotions, I didn't want to leave him. I couldn't lose him again. How could I say goodbye after we just found each other again?

I leaned against his chest, as I watched Sam kiss Rob. She seemed happy and they were talking about when they would see each other again. I knew that Eric would be coming home Friday night but it seemed too long. I felt Eric move me away from his chest, "You have to get back on the road, Gorgeous."

"What? You don't want to hold me anymore?" I smirked at him.

"You know that I could hold you all day long, Emily. Last night was amazing, the start of our new life will continue down that same path, amazing," he said moving my hair behind my ear as he leaned down and kissed my cheek.

I could have melted right there, "I love you, Eric."

He smiled at me and sighed, "I've missed you, Emily. You are back in my life now and I'm not losing you again."

I smiled, "I'm not going anywhere." He leaned down and kissed me again. His lips moved with mine, his scent made me forget where I was, what I was doing. Our lips parted as his tongue found mine. The moan escaped my lips without me even realizing it, just like in high school Eric moved away from my lips just enough to almost growl at me, "You have got to save that moan until we are alone again." He smirked at me as I felt Sam next to me.

I turned to look at her, "Yes?"

"Are we leaving or not?" She smiled.

"Unfortunately, yes," I said turning back to Eric, "I want to see you as soon as you get into town, ok?"

"Of course, Baby. I promise the minute I arrive, I will be at your house." He smiled as he kissed me again.

Sam gave him a hug and said good bye to Rob. As I got into the car and drove away, I could see him watching until we disappeared down the road and that's when the tears started.

I cried on and off for three hours. As we walked into our dorm building, I realized how lonely I was. I felt like I was missing something important in my life. It was so strange, we had been back together for less than twenty four hours but I guess I knew all summer long that I still loved him, I just had to bury the feelings until I healed. Of course having sex with him sprung the emotions right to the top. It was beautiful, emotional and I needed it again as I laughed at myself.

"What's so funny?" Sam asked as she was digging through her desk for something.

"Nothing, just a thought I had." I smirked, "What are you looking for?"

"I'm trying to find my history book I have the exam in the morning."

I got on my knees and looked under my bed then moved to look under her bed, she had a habit of leaving stuff everywhere. I finally found it buried in her laundry pile on the floor. I didn't bother to ask her how it got there.

FALL BREAK

All my mid-terms were over; I could finally relax for the next week before heading back to school. I pulled into my mom's driveway and saw Paul's car there. Mom and Paul have been getting more serious, every time I came home he was there and I could tell how happy my mom was getting. It was adorable.

I grabbed my bags from my car as I headed inside, it would be an hour or so before Eric got into town, so I had time to shower and change. I walked in and didn't hear anything I called for my mom but didn't get a response. I walked around the house and headed to the bedroom seeing the door shut. I stopped dead in my tracks. Oh God!

I quickly turned and ran up the stairs to my bedroom. I wanted to die. Oh no, I'm not going back downstairs. I grabbed my cell phone and dialed Eric as I shut my bedroom door.

"Hey Baby, I'm almost home," He said picking up.

"Eric, oh my God!"

"What's wrong, Emily?" He sounded worried.

"I just heard my mom having sex."

"Eww!"

"I ran upstairs and I'm hiding until its safe again."

He laughed, "I'm about fifteen minutes away, do you want me to come rescue you?"

"Yes please."

We hung up the phone and I raced across the hall into the bathroom and took my shower.

As I finished putting my jeans on, I heard laughing from downstairs. They must be done, Thank God! I grabbed my sweater and headed down the stairs.

"Hey Guys."

My mom jumped up and hugged me, "Emily! When did you get home?"

"Oh, about an hour ago, I didn't want to *disturb* you," I said walking into the kitchen.

My mom followed behind me blushing, "I'm sorry, Sweetie, we were just..celebrating..."

"Celebrating, what?" I asked grabbing a soda from the fridge.

"Well, I have some news," She explained as Paul came into the kitchen, "We got engaged last night."

I dropped my soda can on the floor as it splashed everywhere, "Oh my God, I'm so sorry I will clean that up."

"You ok, Emily?" Mom asked as she grabbed the sponge from my hands.

"I'm just shocked I didn't think you guys were there yet."

Paul smiled, "I love her, Emily. She makes me feel whole again. We have so much in common; our divorces, our work. We just fit together."

My mom smiled from ear to ear as they started to kiss each other, "Please stop that."

Mom laughed as she put her arm around Paul, "Well, you are happy for me, right?"

"Of course Mom, sorry, just shocked," I said moving to give her a big hug, "Paul, welcome to our strange family."

Paul laughed, "Well, I'm looking forward to being your stepfather."

Just what I needed another father. He was nice, I couldn't say anything bad about him, he definitely made my mom happy so who was I to complain? I heard my cell phone ringing as I opened it, "Hey you, you home?"

"Yep and I'm ready to see you, can I come over?" Eric asked.

"Yes, please! Let's get some food."

"I will see you soon."

I hung up and looked at my mom, "Yeah, there is something you should know, Mom."

"What is it, Sweetie?" She started to smile ear to ear, "You saw Eric, didn't you?"

"Yes."

"And?

"We worked things out and we are back together again,"

My mom jumped across the room and threw her arms around me, "That's so wonderful, Emily. I'm so happy for you!"

I smiled at her, "Yeah, he's back in town for a week and heading over right now."

"I can't wait to see him again. Oh, I'm so happy right now. I found the right guy and you are back with your guy. The Stone women are doing alright!"

I laughed as I saw Eric pull into the driveway with his Mustang, I missed that car. I walked to the side door as Eric walked up the sidewalk, "I'm so happy to see you!"

He smiled, "Yeah? How happy?"

I smirked as he got closer and pulled me into his arms, "I will show you later," I smiled, "My mom wants to say hi first."

"Ok, but first," Eric said leaning in and kissing me. His lips felt like heaven on mine, my arms moved around his neck as I pulled him closer to me. My tongue pierced his lips as I found his tongue. I felt his hands moving down my back. I moaned softy as I pulled away from him.

"You are going to be death of me, Gorgeous. Forget your mom; let's go back to my house, my parents are out of town."

I laughed as I pulled him into the house. Paul was sitting on the couch next to my mom, it was so cute, "Mom, someone wanted to say hi."

My mom quickly got off the couch and ran over to hug Eric, "I'm so happy you guys worked this thing out. She was miserable without you, Eric."

I glared at her, "Mom!"

"Well, it's true. She just moped around, crying all the time, tossing in her sleep. It was bad."

I wanted to hurt her, "Are you kidding me right now?"

Eric was laughing, "Well, Mrs. Stone, I was pretty miserable too."

"That's not helping right now, Eric," I said punching his arm.

"She really missed you, Eric. You know how many times I told her to call you but she is so stubborn sometimes."

I looked at them both as they went on and on about me like I wasn't standing there, "Are you two done yet? I'm hungry so I'm going to dinner, if you two would like to continue, I will just leave now."

My mom hugged me as Paul laughed, "She is definitely your daughter," Paul said standing up and walking over to Eric, "Nice to finally meet you, Eric. I've heard a lot about you these past few months."

I blushed again, I couldn't take it as I walked into the kitchen to get a bottle of water. I felt him come up behind me and put his arms around me, "Baby, we were just teasing, you ok?"

I turned around to face him, "Yes, can we please just go?"

He smiled, "Come on, we will go back to my place."

I smiled as he led me outside.

As we walked into his house, it was so quiet. Every time that I have been there, his parents were busy doing something and his siblings were arguing or playing in the game room, but it was quiet. He grabbed my hand and took me into his room. I have been in there before but not for long, his father had a weird thing about me being there.

I walked around his huge room, looking at all his football trophies and jerseys. He had the walls covered with sports posters and pennants. "Are you into the sports or something?" I said laughing at him.

He chuckled, "Yeah, something like that."

I continued to look at his stuff as I came across a photo album sitting on his desk. I grabbed it and started to look through it. I smiled as I saw pictures of our senior year. "Wow, you really kept a lot of our pictures, didn't you?"

He walked over to me and put his arms around me and kissed my neck, "Of course, Gorgeous. Our senior year was the best year of my life, until I messed it up."

I pouted as I looked at our senior prom picture. We looked so good dressed up, he had his arms around me and we both looked so happy. I wanted to cry over the fact that we lost the entire summer. But, it didn't matter now, we found each other again.

"What are you thinking about, Emily?" He whispered in my ear.

"Just us, wishing we didn't lose the entire summer and how we have to be apart from each other just don't seem fair, you know?"

"I know but we will just enjoy our time together now."

I smiled as I turned to face him, he was so handsome I still have no idea why he chose me. I leaned up and kissed his lips. He responded right away by tightening his arms around my waist. I felt his hand slip underneath my sweater and touched my bare skin.

I felt the flames instantly. My skin grew hotter by the minute as he continued to caress me. Our kiss deepened as I heard his moan.

My hands slid underneath his shirt and started to pull it off. He broke the kiss long enough for me to remove it. I smiled as I saw his bare chest, my fingertips running over the firm abs. I bent my head down as I kissed his chest lightly. I felt him respond as he reached for my sweater and pulled it off.

He gasped when he realized that I wasn't wearing anything underneath it, "You really are going to be the death of me, Emily."

I smirked at him as my fingers trembled to undo his jeans. I slid my hands into the waist as I already felt his heat. His lips were moving down the side of my neck touching my shoulder. I couldn't think of anywhere else I wanted to be.

We laid in his bed for the next couple of hours. We were wrapped up in his blankets, cuddling close to each other. This time was definitely better than the last. It seemed that each time we were with each other, it was more intense as we learned what the other person liked and each time we became more connected each other.

I was starting to wake up as I moved my fingertips across his chest. I could feel his grip around me tighten and pull me closer to him, it was dark in the room now as I searched for his lips and found them. His moan made me deepen the kiss as he pulled me on top of him. I could feel every part of his body against mine. The moment happened so fast, I couldn't have stopped it if I wanted to.

"Emily, I love you so much," Eric said in between heavy breaths.

"I love you too please don't ever let me go again."

"Never, as long as I live, you are mine, Emily, only mine." My body responded to his voice, it was deep and dark. I had never heard that tone before and I loved it.

I collapsed on his chest and listened to his heartbeat race. I looked at his alarm clock and it was already eleven at night. I knew I should be heading home shortly, but I didn't want to face the newly engaged couple. I would have rather stayed in Eric's bed all night long.

He rolled me off his chest and onto my side, kissing me the entire movement. I felt so safe in his arms. I suddenly realized I felt very icky, for the lack of a better word.

"Baby, you wanna shower with me, before you take me home?"

He smirked at me, "Your wish is my command."

Wrapped in his towel and walking back into his bedroom, hearing him come behind me. He started kissing my neck slowly, "Eric, this isn't helping, we need to behave."

He laughed as he pulled away and dropped his towel to get changed. I couldn't take my eyes off of him. I sat on his bed and watched him. As his jeans came up and zippered my eyes went back to his. I could see the desire still in him as he pulled me off his bed and released my towel to the floor. He slowly dressed me as he kissed every place he was touching. My head was going to explode, I wanted to tell him to behave himself but I couldn't.

Finally with everything in place, his lips found mine. Breaking away slightly, "Baby, really, we need to go."

He smirked as he grabbed my hand and took me home.

LIFE

When I woke up in the morning, I couldn't help but smile. Last night was wonderful, being in Eric's arms was the only place I wanted to be and right now I was missing him. It all felt like a dream to me, it was a year ago that I had started to date him and now I was in love with him and shared something so special with him.

Though I couldn't help but realize that last night we weren't as careful as we should have been. Eric always took precautions but the moment hit us so fast that we didn't even think about it. I'm sure it's fine, one time isn't going to make a difference, I'm happy right now and I'm not going to ruin it but over-thinking it.

I managed to get out of bed and head into the bathroom. Luckily, last night the newly engaged couple was already in bed. It's not that I'm not happy for them and I honestly don't know why I'm having problems with this. I wonder if she told my father yet.

I headed downstairs in my pajamas hoping to grab a pop tart and head back to my room but no such luck. They were up and making breakfast already.

"Good Morning, Emily," Paul said as he set the table.

"Morning, Paul." I said as I walked into the kitchen. My mom was cooking breakfast I could smell the bacon & eggs as I hugged her. "Wow, breakfast, we still celebrating?"

My mom laughed, "Yes. Come on, grab some food and sit down with us."

I placed the platter in the middle of the table and sat down with the happy couple. Paul started to dig in as my mom talked, "So, Sweetie, we have been talking about the wedding. We definitely want to keep it simple. It's a second wedding for both of us, so nothing big. We were thinking next May. Gives us some time to make adjustments, you know?"

"What kind of adjustments?" I asked worried.

"Well, Paul is going to be moving in, you will be in and out with school and it's going to be an adjustment to get used to everything."

I nodded watching them cuddle next to each other while trying to eat. I kept looking at the wall clock wondering if it was too early to call Eric. I needed an escape. I was so happy for my mom but something just made me feel uncomfortable and I wasn't sure what it was.

I finished my breakfast and headed upstairs to my room. I had a few assignments for school that I needed to do before next week but I wasn't feeling up to it right now. I sat in my window seat and saw that the leaves were changing and the wind was strong today. I watched the orange and red leaves blowing down the street. Grabbing my sketch pad, I heard a soft knock on my door.

"Hey, it's just mom," She said as she came over and sat next to me.

"What's up?"

"I'm getting a vibe that you aren't happy and I wanted to know why."

"It's not that Mom, I'm so happy for you and Paul. I like him, he's very nice and I love seeing you happy again."

"Ok, then what's on your mind?"

"I don't know. I guess I'm just pre-occupied."

She laughed softly, "Eric."

I nodded, "Having him back in my life has been wonderful, Mom. We have really reconnected. I'm back to where I started though, wondering if we can make a long distance relationship work. It's going to start snowing soon and I won't be able to travel that far or he won't be able to get home. It just frankly sucks."

She laughed again and put her hand on my leg, "You will figure it out I have faith in you. You two were meant for each other. Just don't let it affect your schoolwork, ok?"

I nodded, "I know, I really enjoy my classes. I definitely picked the right field."

"I'm happy to hear that, are you and Sam still getting along?"

I laughed, "Yeah, she keeps me on my toes, I'm lucky to have her, Mom."

She nodded and walked over to my desk, "I see you put your pictures back out, I love this one from your prom. That dress was beautiful on you. Maybe we should get you the same color dress for our wedding."

"Red is a great color, it would look great as your colors."

She turned back towards me as she leaned against the desk, "Honey, would you be my maid of honor?"

I smiled and laughed, "Of course, Mom! I would be honored to," I said as I got up and hugged her, "I'm sorry about my mood, I guess I'm just shocked that it happened so fast, but between Dad having a new baby and you getting married, maybe I just felt I was going to be forgotten about."

"Emily, you know in your heart that's not true. You always have a room here plus you now have a step-father that is going to love getting to know you. As far as your father, well, he has his issues, but he's always a phone call away. You know that."

I nodded, "I do. Well, I promise to act more mature about this. I'm glad you came up and talked to me."

She smiled at me and hugged me again, "You know you can always talk to me about anything. I love having you back in my life and now, we get to plan this wedding and have some fun!"

I chuckled, "Yes, I can't wait."

She left my room and heading back downstairs, I went to sit in my window seat again and started reading my textbook. My mind started to drift again to Eric, I missed him. I grabbed my cell phone and dialed him.

"Hello?"

"Hey, it's me," I said smiling out the window.

"Hey you, what's going on?"

"I miss you, you want to see me?"

"Of course, what do you want to do?"

"I could come over I want to take a walk."

"Everything ok?" He asked concerned.

"Yeah, just need some air and a break from wedding central for a bit."

"Ok, well, I just got up, I'm going to hop into the shower, give me an hour?"

"Sure, see you then."

CAUGHT

I changed into jeans and a sweater and took a slow walk over to Eric's. I was happy again.

I walked up his front sidewalk and knocked on his door, his family was still out of town so I didn't have to prepare myself for his father. He was a nice man but he was very protective of Eric's football career. Nothing was going to stand in the way of his son joining the professional league.

The door opened and Eric was standing there, "Hey Gorgeous, come on in."

"Hey, have you missed me?" I smirked at him as he grabbed me and kissed me, "I guess so."

He laughed, "You want me to make you some lunch? I was going to make a sandwich."

"Sure, sounds good, I can help." I followed him into the kitchen. I grabbed the bread from the cupboard as he grabbed the turkey.

"Hey Emily, I wanted to say something about last night," He said reaching for me and pulling me close to his body.

"What's wrong?" I asked concerned.

"Um, I wanted to apologize about my actions. I don't know if you realize it but we didn't take precautions last night. After I left you, I realized that things got passionate very quickly. I can't believe I forgot to protect you."

"Yeah, I realized that this morning. I'm not mad at you, I didn't say anything either. I was taken back by how amazing it was."

He nodded, "Should we be worried?"

"I honestly don't know. I will have to sit down and figure it out. Eric, I'm sure we will be ok. It was one time. I will let you know when I get home."

"Ok, if for any reason something happens, you know I'm by your side, right?"

"Eric, I'm not even going to talk to you about this. There is no need right now."

He laughed, "Ok."

We finished eating and started watching TV. He started flipping through the channels as I snuggled close to him on the couch. I could stay in his arms forever as my head leaned against his firm chest his fingers caressed my bare back underneath my sweater.

"I love you, Eric," I whispered to him.

"I love you too, Baby. I don't know what I'm going to do when I leave in a few days. Can I take you with me?"

I laughed, "You can stash me away in your suitcase."

He laughed, "Come here, Gorgeous."

I moved so I could face him as his lips touched mine. I crawled across his lap as I straddled his hips. I heard my favorite moan as I deepened the kiss. I felt his hands move under my sweater as I lifted my arms as he removed it.

His lips moved to my neck as his hands traced over my lacy bra. I moaned softly, "God Eric, I want you right now."

He quickly responded as he pushed me back onto the couch and laid on top of me. His fingers quickly unzipped my jeans and my fingertips quickly found his abs which was my favorite part of his body. I slide his shirt off and threw it across the room, "I don't like when you wear shirts I miss the view too much."

He laughed, "I will never wear another one again."

"Wait, I change my mind, you have to wear one in public because I don't think I want every girl seeing what is mine, so just around me, no shirts."

He laughed louder, "You got it, Baby." He moved back to my lips as his body moved with mine, my hands undid his jeans as we heard a sound coming through the front door.

"Oh crap, grab your shirt, Emily, my parents are home," He quickly jumped off of me as I reached for my shirt on the ground but it was too late, his parents were already in the living room staring at me.

"Eric, do you mind explaining to me what the hell you are doing?" His father yelled at him. His mom quickly came over to me and pulled me into the kitchen.

"I'm so sorry, Mrs. Mason. I normally don't behave like this."

She nodded, "Emily, I understand, you guys are in college now, you are back together, you were happy to see each other, but we do have rules in this house.

"I realize that, Mrs. Mason. I'm so sorry again," I said as I looked back into the living room and saw Eric and his father having a screaming match. I was starting to feel very uncomfortable, "I think I will walk home, I will just go out the back door."

"Emily, I think I have to tell your mother, she's a good friend of mine and she deserves to know what is going on in her daughter's life."

I stopped in my tracks, my mind started racing. I turned back to look at her, "Is there anyway you would let me do that. She's still celebrating her engagement and I really don't want to upset her right now."

She stared at me, "Well, ok, I will talk to her tomorrow though Emily, so make sure you tell her tonight. I will call her to congratulate her."

I nodded and walked out the back door hearing the last of the screaming. The whole way home I kept trying to think of a way to tell my mom that I was just caught about to have sex with Eric. I walked into the house and saw them sitting on the couch watching TV.

"Hey honey, back so soon? What's going on?" She said leaving Paul and joining me in the kitchen. "Mom, I need to talk to you about something."

She sat down and looked at me, "What's wrong? Did you guys break up again?"

"No, nothing like that yet," I said sitting down next to her, "I don't know how to say this."

"Honey, just tell me, I'm your mother, you can tell me anything," She said grabbing my hand looking very concerned.

"Mom, Eric and I have had sex."

She just looked at me, no words came out of her mouth she just stared at me, "Well, you are nineteen now. I'm not totally surprised but please tell me that you are being safe about this because I'm not ready to be a grandmother yet."

I looked at her thinking about the one time we weren't safe, "Well, for the most part we have been, but there was one time that we both got lost in the moment and we both forgot."

She sighed, "Please tell me that you aren't pregnant, Emily. You just started college, you aren't ready for that yet, believe me."

"I know Mom and as far as I'm aware I'm not, so don't worry about that."

"You need to worry about it, Emily. This is very serious."

"Mom, there is something else," I said looking at her, seeing her stern face.

"What Emily?"

"I was just over at Eric's and his parents came home early," I said as my voice trailed off.

"Oh God Emily, are you serious? She is my friend, I need to call her and apologize for your actions. I'm so embarrassed."

"I'm so sorry, Mom, I really didn't mean to hurt you. Please don't be upset with me."

"Emily, I need you to go into your room for awhile. I'm so disappointed with you right now."

I nodded as I left the room and ran up the stairs and shut my bedroom door. I reached for my cell phone to text Eric to see if he was surviving his screaming match with his father. I quickly got a response saying he was locked in his room because he couldn't listen to his father anymore.

I sighed as I wrote back saying I was in the same place. I laid back on my bed and just wanted to go back to school. I shouldn't feel ashamed, I'm nineteen, I'm already in college, I'm an adult, why is she making me feel like I shamed her. I heard my phone beep again as Eric responded saying he was sneaking out and he would be waiting for me at the corner store if I could get away. I didn't know how to respond, my mother would kill me if she caught me but I needed to see him.

I quickly responded saying I would see him there. I headed out of my bedroom and quietly walked down the stairs. I heard yelling from my mom directed at Paul. She was screaming that she taught me better than this, she wasn't upset that I had sex but she was upset that I was so careless about it. Paul was defending me, I was shocked. He was trying to explain to my mom that kids will be kids that they just have to stand by me. I was starting to feel guilty about sneaking out, but I needed to see Eric.

I opened up the front door quietly and ran down the front sidewalk and quickly turned the corner and was out of sight from the house. As I walked down the street, I could see Eric waiting for me at the corner I ran over to him and threw my arms around him.

"I'm so sorry, Emily. I really messed things up," He said as he kissed the top of my head.

"Don't be sorry, Eric. It's our parents not us. I don't feel like we did anything wrong. I love you and I want to spend my life with you and what we did comes along with it. Yeah, it sucks that our parents found out this way but we can't change that now."

He nodded, "Come on, let's go somewhere quieter." He opened the door for me and we drove off.

We ended up at my dorm room. I smiled seeing Sam's clothes all over her bed, apparently she forgot to take her laundry home with her.

"So, this is your room, huh?" He said walking over to my desk, looking through my literature books. He grabbed a picture frame that I had on my desk. It was from homecoming, taken in my mother's living room. He smiled as he thought back to that evening, "Amazing how in a year things have changed, huh?"

I smirked at him as I walked over and wrapped my arms around him, "I love you, Honey."

He put the frame down and wrapped his arms around me, "I love you too, Gorgeous."

I don't remember when the tears started but they were flowing very easily now.

"Baby, are you crying?" He asked as he pulled away and looked into my eyes, "Emily, please, you are breaking my heart," He said wiping my cheeks.

"I'm just so worried about my Mom; she is so upset with me. I had to tell her that we had sex without protection and she lost it."

He nodded, "Yeah, my Father said I'm thinking with my male appendage, to phrase it nicely and not my brain."

I chuckled a little, "I guess we should talk about the chance that I could be pregnant."

He put his arms around me, "If you are, we deal with it. I'm not going anywhere, Emily. You are my life now, I lost you once and I won't let that happen again."

"What about our parents?"

"My mother will always be there for us, now my Father may be a different story. He has already threatened to pull me off the football team if I continue to see you."

"WHAT!" I yelled at him and walked across the room, "Eric, you are going to lose the most important thing in your life because of me."

He walked over and spun me around to face him as he placed his hands on both sides of my face and looked at me, "You are the most important thing in my life, now and forever. If I blow out my knee tomorrow in practice, I will still have you there to take care of me, Emily. When will you realize that we will be together forever?"

I looked into his eyes, they were intense, he wasn't even blinking, I leaned in and kissed his lips with every ounce of passion that I had. He quickly responded wrapping his arms around me. I felt his tongue open my lips and find mine. My fingers ran through his hair, pulling his face tighter against mine.

He pulled away suddenly, "I don't think it's a good time to start this," He said smiling at me.

I nodded, "We should probably head home, I'm sure my mother is going to kill me."

He looked at me, "If it gets really bad, just text me and I will be there before you know it."

I nodded, "I'm sure you will have your own problems." We headed out the door and towards home to face our growing problems.

THE TRUTH

As we pulled into the driveway I could see the lights in my living room still on. I knew she was waiting up for me. I sighed softly.

"Just remember if it gets really bad, I will come back, Emily, just call me," He said kissing me lightly. I nodded as I get out of his car and walked into the house.

My mom was waiting in the living room, staring at the door waiting for me to walk into the room. She didn't say anything, she just looked at me.

I opened my mouth to tell her that I was sorry but she spoke first, "Emily, you have never been a problem child. You have always been there when I needed you and I know that it's been a transition for both of us when you moved back here but I always trusted you and knew you were always going make the right choices because that's how I raised you. But, when I walked into your bedroom and saw that you left. I can't put into words how mad I felt," She said stood up and walked over to me, "Emily, I know you are nineteen and feel like you know what is right for you, but you are still very young and starting to stray off the right path."

I watched her as she talked to me I could see she was really upset, I wasn't used to feeling this way. I could feel the tears form in my eyes, "I'm so sorry, Mom. I hate being a disappointment to you but I need you to realize that Eric is the biggest thing in my life right now. I can't be without him, we both experienced what that is like and I don't want to feel that again."

"I can't even begin to run through the list of things in my head that we need to discuss. I was a teenager once, Emily, I know what first love feels like, I know the power of it, the emotions of it but you also need to realize the responsibility of entering into a sexual relationship. I'm not stupid, Emily, I had sex as a teenager also, I was also stupid about it," She looked at me as she put her hands on my shoulders, she started to cry, "I had to make a very tough choice when I became pregnant at eighteen. You can't even imagine how it feels to make a decision like that, your grandparents did not understand and I missed my high school graduation. I was so ashamed of the mess that I had made, after giving up that baby I had to leave town, I couldn't stand seeing the disappointment in my father's eyes. So, I ended up in Texas, getting my GED and going to school. I never wanted to tell you but I guess I should have, maybe it would have changed your mind about sex."

Paul walked over to my mom and took her into his arms. I couldn't believe what I just heard my mom had to give up a baby. She was even younger than me when she had to make that choice. She cried into Paul's chest, "Em, I'm going to take your mom into the bedroom for awhile, she needs to relax. Stay here, ok? I will be right back."

I nodded as he walked from the room, I felt my phone vibrate in my pocket as I looked to see Eric's message. He typed; *my father is sending me back to Syracuse early. I have to leave the house tonight. He doesn't want me to see you anymore. We need to talk.* I quickly typed back before Paul returned; *you can't leave without seeing me first. But I can't leave right now. My mother is having a break down. Please just wait for me to text you back before you leave town.*

Paul walked back into the room, "I know that I have no right as your future step-father to discuss any of this with you, but I just wanted you to know that your mother just wants the best for you. She is so scared that you will go down the same path that she did and she wants better for you."

"I know that, Paul. I feel so horrible about hurting her the way I have. I didn't realize my relationship would do this to her."

"I think the shock of actually knowing that you are having sex is hard for her. She is so worried about you taking risks but I know how is happens. I was a teenager a long time ago but it was the same way. The moment happens, you don't think about it but there are consequences."

I cringed, I know he means well but I don't feel comfortable talking to him about this, "Thanks Paul, I will talk to her once she calms down."

He nodded, "Why don't you head up to bed, you guys can talk in the morning."

I nodded as I left the room, I grabbed my phone and called Eric, he answered quickly, "Where are you, Em?"

"In my room, there is no way I can leave right now, my mom is having a nervous breakdown."

"I'm going to stay at Todd's house tonight so don't worry about it, we can see each other tomorrow."

"I'm so scared, Eric. Your father doesn't want us together and my mom is going crazy because she thinks her daughter is knocked up. I can't lose you again. I just can't," I said trying to keep my voice low but the tears were coming fast.

"Emily, look out your window." I went to my window seat and saw his car parked just past the tree line. He was leaning against the side of it, staring up into the window, "I love you, Emily. We are not breaking up; we are just going to have to figure out a way around this."

"I love you, too, Eric but what if I am pregnant? I'm not worried about diseases, I know you and you know you were my one and only. So, my mom can calm down about that. But, she told me tonight that she had to get up a baby. She's so stressed out that I am pregnant," I said watching him stare at me.

He sighed, as much I hated to have him do that I loved the sound of it, I was so madly in love with him, "Em, if you are, we will have to come to a decision but until then, we will just have to go on. I'm not leaving you no matter what, my father can rant and rave but at the end of the day, you will be mine."

I knew he couldn't see me that well but I smiled hearing that.
"I wish I could kiss you right now."

He laughed, "Me too, Gorgeous."

"I think I need to go talk to my mom, Eric. Call me or text me later, ok?"

"Of course, I won't leave until we see each other, so please don't worry about that, ok?"

"Yeah, talk later." As we hung up I waved at him as he waved back. I headed downstairs to find my mom. She was in the kitchen drinking a cup of coffee, her eyes still puffy.

"Mom?" I asked testing the water.

"Hey, sit down," She said waving to the chair next to her.

"Is it ok to talk with you?"

"Of course, Em, You can always talk to me. I know my emotions get the best of me but I'm ok now. What do you want to talk about?"

"Well, first, I know it was tough for you to tell me that story. I wanted to thank you for telling me though. It gives me a lot to think about, I'm not going to just blow it off." She smiled at me, "Second, I'm not late yet, Mom. So, don't stress out about me being pregnant. There is no need right now. I know when Eric and I decided to have sex, there is a huge responsibility with it, and I'm not stupid. Our emotions got the better of us one time."

She nodded and I knew she knew what I was talking about. She was trying to be understanding, "Emily, I know you are about to turn twenty and you have your whole life in front of you. I don't want to tell you how to live your life, I just want to guide you in the right direction. I see how you look at Eric, I saw it that morning he came over here for breakfast," She reached for my hand and gently grabbed it, "You are in love, I see that and I accept it. I'm not going to forbid you to see him because I know the effects of that too."

I laughed, "Well, you don't have to worry about that. Eric's dad kicked him out of the house tonight and I'm not allowed around him anymore."

My mom let go of my hand and stared at me, "Are you serious?"

I nodded, "Yeah, he's pretty ticked off about everything."

"He's not driving back to Syracuse tonight, right?"

I shook my head, "No, he's staying at a friend's house tonight."

She smiled, "Ok, good," She said as she went back to her coffee.

"Thank you for caring about him, Mom. That means a lot to me, especially after tonight."

She smiled, "I told you, Em, I have been there before I know exactly where you are right now. You want to be with him all the time. You are afraid of losing him you want to share everything with him."

She did know exactly how I was feeling, "Maybe when things have calmed down a little bit, you can tell me your whole story. I would be interested in knowing it."

She nodded, "Someday."

I got up and kissed her cheek, "Thank you for being the best mother ever."

She chuckled, "You are still in trouble, Emily. Don't think you are avoiding it. You snuck out, you embarrassed me in front of Eric's parents and you were very foolish about your sexual decisions."

I sighed, "I know, in two days, I head back to college and will be out of your hair for awhile."

She laughed, "We will talk tomorrow, why don't you head to bed."

"Night, Mom." I headed upstairs and went into my bedroom. I sat in my window seat and called Eric.

"Hey Baby, how's home life going?"

I smiled, "It's actually ok. She pissed off but she's dealing with it."

"At least one parent is reasonable."

"She was worried about you, wanted to make sure you weren't driving back to Syracuse just shows me that she still wants us to be happy. She's just not happy that I decided to start a sexual relationship with you."

"Does it count that I'm happy you did?"

I laughed, "Yeah, I'm happy too. So, what are we going to do, Eric? I mean, you are heading back tomorrow I'm going back in the next couple of days. How are we going to handle this?"

"Well, I'm hoping that you can come out and see me whenever you can and I will come home whenever I can but you have to remember, my father can't know anything. He's threatened to pull me out of Syracuse and end my football career."

"Eric, we can't let that happen!"

"Emily, calm down. Nothing is going to happen to me if we keep our relationship quiet."

I sighed, "I want to see you."

"Can you leave the house?"

"No, I better not chance it tonight seeing that we left on a positive note. I would like to keep it that way."

"Well then, I will see you in the morning before I leave ok?"

"Yeah, call me and wake me up."

"Ok, sweet dreams, Emily. I love you."

"I love you too, Eric. Dream of me."

"I always do."

PROPOSAL

The morning came quick. I woke up and stared out the window for a long time before I got up and walked into the bathroom. I looked into the mirror and went over the events from the night before.

My mind raced about not wanting to go downstairs. I wasn't sure what was waiting for me. Last night my mom was so upset and Eric was kicked out of his house. I wasn't sure which problem I should deal with first.

I headed downstairs and saw that Paul was sitting on the couch reading the morning paper.

"Morning, Emily, sleep well?" He said putting the paper down.

I nodded, "Is Mom up yet?"

He shook his head, "No, she went to bed late last night. I don't want to wake her up yet."

I nodded, "Ok, well I'm going to go outside for a second."

I walked out the front door and grabbed my cell phone I quickly dialed Eric, "Hey Baby."

"Em, I need to see you soon, I need to hit the road, my Dad found out that I stayed at Todd's house last night and he's pissed off."

I sighed listening to him, "Ok, can you come over now and see me?"

"Yes, I'm about to turn the corner now, are you outside?"

"Yea, I'll be waiting." I said as I closed my phone and saw him pull into my driveway. I ran over to his car and slid into the passenger seat, his lips were quickly on mine. I lost myself in his kiss. I felt his anger, worry and love for me. Our lips parted as our tongues found each other, his fingers dug into my hair. I moaned softly, knowing I had to pull away.

I looked up into his eyes, "Hey you."

He didn't say anything to me, but I could see the worry in his eyes, "Hey."

"So, what's the plan?"

"I don't know but I have to leave. Todd said that my dad is looking for me so I need to hit the road before he finds me. I need to let him to cool down before I lose my mind. Emily, this isn't going to be pretty. This is why I didn't have a girlfriend in high school until you came along but God, the minute I saw you, I know I had to take the chance and I will never look back."

I smiled at him, "I feel the same way, Eric. You are my life, my love and I will fight for us until I stop breathing."

He smiled at me, "Marry me."

I just looked at him, my mouth opened. My heart stopped. He's crazy, he's not thinking right, how could he ask me that? "Eric."

"I'm serious, Emily. You are my world. No one can stand between us. Marry me, we will be together forever."

"Baby, you know that I want to spend the rest of our lives together, but we are freshman in college, you have a career in front of you and most importantly our parents would kill us."

He just smiled at me, "Emily Stone, be my wife."

I just stared at him I couldn't answer him right away. I didn't know what to say, this was a big deal. Was he serious?

"I know I don't have a ring and I know you have no idea what to say, so I won't force it. Just remember it and when you are ready, you just have to say yes."

I nodded as I started to cry, his lips found mine again. I couldn't let him go but I knew I had too, "You better hit the road, call me when you get there, I have to go deal with my own problems."

He nodded as he kissed me again, "I love you, Gorgeous."

"I love you too, Baby," I smiled, "Forever."

When I walked back into the house, my mom was up and making breakfast. I couldn't help but think that I was just proposed to, I couldn't stop smiling.

"Good Morning, Mom."

She turned quickly and hugged me, "Emily, I love you, you know that, right?"

I smiled, "Of course, Mom. I'm sorry about yesterday. I wish that all happened differently."

She nodded, "Me too. But we just have to deal with it now. First things first, we need to make sure you aren't pregnant."

"Mom, I'm sure I'm not. But, I will call the Dr and see if I can get in next week, ok?"

She nodded, "Ok. That's fine. What about you and Eric?"

"What about us?" I asked sitting down at the breakfast table.

"Well, has he gone back to school? I saw that he was here, how are his parents?"

I sighed, "It's pretty bad right now. His father is threatening to pull him off the team and kicked him out of the house."

She nodded, "Yeah, I'm not surprised, is he ok?"

"He's upset but figures things will calm down again, but he feels we may need to take a break so his father doesn't blow a gasket."

"I'm sorry, Em. I know he means a lot to you and this isn't what you wanted."

"Definitely not but I will talk to him later once things calm down."

She nodded, "When are you heading back to school?"

"I think tonight. Sam is going to be there, figured I need some time to get back into the swing of it."

"Ok, just say good bye before you leave," She said as she left the room.

BACK TO SCHOOL

I arrived back to school and Sam was already there, she ran over and hugged me, "I missed you, Em. What's going on?"

I couldn't help but laugh a little as I placed my bags on my bed, "Oh, it was a busy week."

Sam grabbed her chair and sat down, "Well, tell me, I feel out of the loop since I was on vacation with my mom, I haven't talked to you."

I sat down on my bed and started to open up about the incident with Eric's parents and the maybe pregnancy, ending with the story about my mom. Sam sat there and listened to the whole story before reacting in anyway.

"So, that was my week of hell, how was your vacation?" I laughed as I put my head into my hands.

Sam got up and sat down next to me and put her arm around me, "Em, listen to me. You will be just fine. Things seem worse than they are and you just need to clear your head. Let's go down to The Union and grab some food." Sam laughed, "You know, you could be eating for two now."

I gasped as I hit her arm, "Not funny, Sam!"

As we walked through campus, I couldn't help but think of Eric and the proposal. I didn't mention it to Sam because I honestly didn't know what to make of it yet. I felt my phone vibrate as I looked down and saw Eric texting me that he loved me. I smiled as I quickly typed him back.

"So, Emily, what are you going to do if you are pregnant? I mean, are you going to keep it?"

"I don't know, I can't think about it. I'm barely half way through my first year of college. My mom will kill me and Eric's parents will kill him. It's too much to think about."

Sam tried to smile at me but I could tell she was worried about me, "Did you call the doctor yet?"

"Not yet, I don't want to do it unless I'm late."

"When are you late?"

I stopped in my tracks as I did the math, "A week, at most."

Sam sighed, "Em. You really need to start thinking about this. At least have an idea in your head of how you will deal with this."

I nodded as we continued through The Union. How could I let this happen? I couldn't stop daydreaming until I heard Sam gasp.

"What?" I looked at her in surprised.

"Emily Stone! Your birthday is in two days! Why didn't you remind me?"

"Oh. That. It's ok, really. There is a lot going on, I forgot."

"We are not forgetting your birthday, Em. You are turning twenty! What do you want to do?"

"Go to Syracuse?" I said half smiling, hoping she would be on board and of course, I should have known better, "Of course! Call him and tell him we are coming out on Saturday."

I smiled as I dialed his number, he quickly picked up, "Hey, Gorgeous."

"Hey Eric. So, in case you didn't notice, my birthday is coming up."

"I know I already have your gift."

"You do? What is it?" I asked smiling.

"I'm not telling you, Gorgeous. Where's the fun in that?"

I laughed, "Well, Sam's gift to me is a trip to Syracuse on Saturday. Interested in seeing me?"

"YES!" He screamed into the phone as Sam grabbed the phone from me.

"Eric, make dinner plans somewhere nice. We will do a group date, I will call Rob and tell him too."

"Sounds great, Sam. Rob was just talking about you. Honestly, I'm sick of hearing about you." He laughed.

"He's so sweet, I miss him. I saw him once over break and can't wait to see him again." She smiled, "See you Saturday."

It was tough getting through the week, but classes were keeping me busy and keeping my mind off my pending problems. Every night I talked with Eric on the phone or computer until I fell asleep. He had informed his father that we had broken up and he was taking his football career serious now, which got his father off his back for at least the moment.

I made an appointment at the campus clinic for Friday afternoon so I could get everyone off my back, my mom has been calling me every day to make sure I don't forget to go.

At the end of my computer class Friday afternoon, I headed over to the clinic, I saw Sam sitting on the bench waiting for me. "Sam, you didn't have to come."

"Of course I did. You are like my sister, I want to make sure everything is ok with you."

I smiled at her, "Thank you."

We walked in and sat in the waiting room, I watched the other people come and go, head colds, broken bones but I seemed to be the only person there that had a worried look on their face.

"Emily Stone?" the nurse asked as she came into the waiting room. I left my stuff with Sam as she wished me good luck and the nurse took me into the back room.

I did all the testing that the doctor wanted to put me through and sat at the small table in the room and waited for him to return. I looked around the room and read the posters, amazing how many diseases are in the world. I laughed trying to keep my mind off of the fact that I'm waiting to find out if I'm pregnant. What would I do? If I am pregnant, I couldn't tell Eric, could I? He would give up football, he would lose his relationship with his father and he would insist on the marriage.

I shook my head, no, I'm not pregnant, and I'm not thinking that way, not yet. I need to calm down and wait for the doctor. As I sat there and waited, the door finally cracked open and Dr. Fisher walked in.

"Ok, Emily, tests are back." He said as he sat down and pulled out the paperwork, my stomach tightened, I felt like I wanted to throw up, this was the moment.

He scanned through the folder and looked up at me, "You're pregnant."

My heart stopped. My world collapsed in on me. He was lying to me, I couldn't be pregnant, not the one time I wasn't protected, this couldn't happen. Then the world faded black.

When I woke up, I was still in the doctor's office. I blinked a few times and felt someone squeeze my hand. I looked over to my left and saw Sam smiling at me, "What happened, Sam?"

"You passed out. You've been out for about ten minutes. The nurse is coming in right now to check on you."

As the nurse ran her tests and I just laid there. I can't believe I passed out. I was just told that I'm pregnant and that my life was now over. I looked over at Sam, who continued to smile, "Do you know?"

Sam smiled, "Not in so many words, but you passed out, Em. I can put the pieces together. It will be ok, we will go back to the room and figure out what to do next."

I nodded as I closed my eyes again. The nurse said that everything seemed ok, she gave me some literature on pregnancy and told me to set up an appointment with my OB-GYN as soon as I could. I nodded as I grabbed the paperwork and headed back to our dorm room.

As soon as we walked in, the tears started to flow. I couldn't stop crying for the next hour and Sam just let me. She held me and kept telling me that things would be ok and she would help with whatever I needed.

I finally fell asleep around one in the morning after talking through all the issues in my head. I was leaving in the morning to see Eric for my birthday dinner and somehow I needed to figure out how to tell him.

LIFE DECISIONS

Sam parked the car at Syracuse University and we headed to Eric's dorm room. She still wanted to do the fancy dinner so I bought along my gown from the prom with my overnight clothes. My heart raced as we got closer to the building. I felt Sam stop and look at me.

"Are you going to be alright? You haven't spoken in the past hour, Em?"

I nodded, "I just don't know what to say to him. I'm about to change his life. He thinks we are about to have this great night and he has no idea that I'm pregnant. How do you tell someone that?"

I heard her sigh, "You just have to tell him the truth. Tell him that you don't expect him to drop out of college, tell him that you want his life to continue, that you are willing to sacrifice everything for him."

I closed my eyes as the tears started again, "Sam, I didn't want this to happen. A year ago, we were in high school, we were worried about what college to pick, I was nervous about my first date with Eric, we were being kids. I'm still a kid!"

Sam hugged me tight as she wiped my tears away, "Come on, he's waiting to see you. You will figure it out as we go through the night. Let's celebrate your birthday."

I smiled as we headed inside, we barely knocked on his door as the door flew open and Eric grabbed me. Feeling his lips on mine never gets old, the kiss deepened as I heard Sam cough behind me.

I smiled as I broke the kiss and looked at Eric, "Hey Handsome."

"Hey Gorgeous. Hey Sam."

"What's up, Eric?" Sam asked coming inside and dumping all the bags on his bed, "I'm just saying hi, I want to see Rob so I'm going to run down to his dorm and leave you two love birds alone for awhile." She kissed Eric on the cheek and left.

Eric grabbed me and pulled me to bed. His lips quickly found mine again, "I love you, Emily."

"I love you too, Eric, so tell me where we are going tonight?"

He smiled, "There is a nice restaurant downtown that I made reservations for and thought the four of us would enjoy it."

"Sounds great," I bit my lip as I cuddled next to him, still couldn't think of the right words to even bring up the subject to him, "So, how are things with your dad?"

"They are ok, he called last night and said he was coming next weekend to visit with my sister." He smiled but I could see the whole situation upset him, "I hate lying to him, but I'm not losing you."

I frowned, "Eric, maybe we need to discuss this more." He quickly cut me off, "No, we aren't discussing this, Emily. I already proposed to you, I'm not living my life without you again. We will just figure this whole thing out."

I quickly calmed him down by kissing him softly, "It's ok." I stood up and walked around the room, looking at his text books and seeing what he was studying. I felt his eyes on me the whole time, "Emily, do you want to tell me something?"

I stopped and turned around slowly, "How do you know that?" He smiled at me and laughed, "We have known each other for over a year now and I think I can tell you have something on your mind."

I kept quiet, this wasn't the time. I didn't know what to say to change the subject either, "I'm fine."

Eric got up and wrapped his arms around me, I felt his breathe on my neck as he stood behind me, "Please tell me."

I softly sighed, my lips opened as the door burst open and in walked Sam and Rob. Thank God.

"Hey Emily!" Rob said giving me a quick hug.

"Hey Rob, what's going on?"

"I wanted to say hi before we started to get ready for tonight, happy birthday, by the way!"

"Thanks. It should be a fun night."

He quickly grabbed Sam and kissed her, "I'm going to head and get in my suit, I'm sure you ladies need to get dressed."

Sam grabbed our bags and headed to the ladies room. I smiled as I turned to Eric, "We will chat later, don't worry. I better go with her." He leaned over and kissed me lightly.

I found Sam in front of the mirror doing her makeup, "So, did you tell him?"

I chuckled, "No, I was about to when you guys came into the room."

"Oh, sorry."

"It's ok, I really didn't want to tell him yet, so not a problem," I smiled as I grabbed my make up from her.

As we did our make-up and got our dresses on, we chatted about the evening and if and when I would tell Eric about the pregnancy. As we finished up, I looked in the mirror and had a flashback to prom night. The same red dress clung to my body just like it did last June. I smiled but quickly it faded as my mind started to think about how my body was going to change. My hands ran down my body and over my stomach. I let out a soft sigh, "Things are going to change, Sam."

Sam stopped checking herself out in the mirror and looked at me, "Emily, please, not tonight. Let's enjoy ourselves. You look hot! Eric is going to lose his mind. Just have a fun birthday and we can get through the rest later, ok?"

I nodded, "I know. Are you ready?"

"Yes, I am, do I look hot?" She asked looking gorgeous in her long gown showing off her long legs with slits in each sides.

"Of course you do, come on, the guys are waiting."

As we walked into the room, the guys were waiting for us to return, Eric smiled and winked at me as I could see the flashback to prom in his eyes, "I love that dress," He smiled as his arms went around me and whispered in the ear, "I promise I won't mess up the evening this time." I smirked as I thought, no but I probably will.

Eric showed us the sights of Syracuse as we drove to the restaurant. When we arrived the boys opened doors for us and ordered for us and treated the evening like we were royalty. We laughed and ate. Eric, Sam & I filled Rob in about high school and all the events that led to our relationship. As we finished up dinner, out of the corner of my eye, I saw candles. The waiters started singing as the cake approached the table. I smiled and it was time for my wish.

Sam looked at me like she knew what my wish was already, Eric and Rob cheered me on as I closed my eyes and wished for God to present the right time to tell Eric that his life was changing forever.

As we left the restaurant and returned to campus, Rob and Sam took off for a walk and Eric took me to back to the room.

When we entered the room, he pulled me into his arms and lightly kissed me, "Happy Birthday, Emily."

I smiled, "Thank you, Handsome." I walked over to his window and looked up at the moon.

"Emily, please tell what is on your mind."

I took a deep breathe as I turned around and looked into his eyes, I was lost in them as always.

He put his hands on my shoulders, "Whatever it is, tell me."

I softly said, "I'm pregnant, Eric. I know this changes everything. I know you must be so upset right now. How are we going to handle this? What about football? What about your parents? What about my parents?" I stopped and just watched his face change. I couldn't read it, "Please say something."

He looked at the floor but slowly looked up into my eyes, "Marry me, Emily."

I couldn't breathe, he didn't overact, he didn't scream at me, he proposed to me again. I tried to catch my breath as my thoughts raced through my head. Through the tears, I responded,

"Yes."

THE END.

CPSIA information can be obtained at www.ICGtesting.com
Printed in the USA
LVOW05s2140251213

366794LV00007B/42/P